Forty South Short Story Anthology 2021

THE TEN BEST ENTRIES FROM THE TASMANIAN WRITERS' PRIZE 2021

Selected by

HILARY BURDEN   CHRIS GALLAGHER   PENNY LANE

40

Editor: Chris Champion
Layout and design: Forty South Publishing Pty Ltd

Publisher: Forty South Publishing Pty Ltd
Hobart, Tasmania
fortysouth.com.au

Printer: IngramSpark

Cover: Waves on rock in Marshall Bay, Flinders Island
Photo by Don Defenderfer,
author of *Tasmania: An island dream* (Forty South Publishing)

Contents

The Tasmanian Writers' Prize

The Tasmanian Writers' Prize began in 2009 and, in order to promote and support writers, each year Forty South has published the winning story in *FortySouth* and produced an annual anthology of the best entries. Since 2014 the competition has been themed on the concept of 'island' and is open to residents of Australia and New Zealand.

WINNERS OF THE TASMANIAN WRITERS' PRIZE

2009 (2010 anthology)	John Hale (TAS)	Ferry
2010 (2011 anthology)	Leigh Swinbourne (TAS)	Away
2011 (2012 anthology)	Kate Esser (TAS)	Crossing water
2013	Debi Hamilton (VIC)	Mud flats
2014	Polly Whittington (TAS)	The chimney pot
2015	Rachel Leary (VIC)	A concrete Aborigine
2016	Craig Cormick (ACT)	No man is an island
2017	Jennifer Porter (VIC)	The Reverend
2018	Melissa Manning (VIC)	Boy
2019	Greg Burgess (TAS)	Pilgrims
2020	Andrea McMahon (TAS)	Damselfly
2021	RI Quin (QLD)	Saving Daniel

To order copies of the anthologies or to view other
Forty South Publishing titles visit:
fortysouth.com.au and go to our FortySouth Bookshop
Email: accounts@fortysouth.com.au
Post: PO Box 168 Lindisfarne TAS 7015

The judges

HILARY BURDEN is a British/Australian author, journalist and photographer. She lives and writes from a shack on an acre in the low hills of Swansea. Her memoir, *A Story of Seven Summers — Life in the Nuns' House*, was published in 2012 by Allen & Unwin.

CHRIS GALLAGHER is an arts manager and festival director and is currently undertaking a Diploma in Sustainability at the University of Tasmania. She was the director of the Tasmanian Writers Centre and the Tasmanian Writers and Readers Festival from 2008-17. Previous to this she was a film and television producer, moving between Melbourne, Sydney and Hobart. She was inspired to move to Tasmania after working on the feature film *The Tale of Ruby Rose* as the production manager.

After a teaching career in Hobart, Canberra and Sydney, during which she wrote two books about teaching, PENNY LANE turned to writing short stories and, more recently poetry, and has won several awards for both stories and poems. She was a finalist in the 2017 Newcastle Poetry Prize, and more recently won first and third prizes in the free verse section of the 2019-20 Sutherland Shire Literary Competition. She has published a Kindle e-book, *Winning Writing: What Works For Me*, about her short story writing.

Foreword

Island: a word to stir imaginings.

Imagine yourself one warm, still day on an island shore. Imagine roaming a grassy headland, passing middened dunes, walking a beach with tidal etchings, all the while revelling in island loveliness. Imagine paddling in green shallows over sand, then swimming at the edge of an immense spread of ocean.

Ocean: the sound of the word is the sound of the ocean itself.

It is the ocean which defines our place in the world, for we live in Oceania, a scattering of thousands of islands and a continent which, rimmed with coastline, is island-like. Ours is a region of island and ocean stories, real and imagined.

Island resonance: words that inspired the writers of 96 short stories entered into the Tasmanian Writers' Prize 2021. Their stories enabled the three judges to traverse islands and seas as we read, reread and discussed the entries. It was an enthralling, thought-provoking adventure, so thank you to every entrant.

Oceania has islands that are idyllic, islands that are exotic, islands that offer sanctuary and respite, islands with enticing opportunities for outdoor leisure and adventure. There's Norfolk Island, where you can stand on an easily accessible peak on a calm day brimming with sunshine, look out to 360 degrees of ocean and feel the exhilaration of a sense of islandness.

Then there is Nauru. There are Manus and Christmas Islands.

There are islands with tragic histories of invasion and devastation.

Whether idyllic or scarred with wretchedness, what all our islands share is the ocean that surrounds them. On a bleak, wind-scoured day, standing on that Norfolk Island peak, you can sense the ocean's menace. And every day there, no matter the weather, on low land beside the sea, there's a convict-era cemetery with so many headstones inscribed *drowned aged 26, drowned aged 27, drowned aged 22*. The potential of the ocean's ferocity is always island-side.

Yet desperate people brave oceans. Some of them feature in our winning story, *Saving Daniel*, a story well worth telling, a story to reflect upon, a beautifully written story with a powerful storyline and poignant moments. Even after several readings during the judging process, the story did not lose its lustre.

The setting for the commended story, *Chasing the light*, is a precarious island coast, a place befitting the story that is told. This story has beguiling language and striking imagery.

Each of these two stories has a strong island resonance, a compelling narrative voice, depth to the central characters, a clear, consistent focus and layers of complexity.

Island: is land. And more besides. Islands are not only geographical entities, but can be each one of us. Islands can imply disconnection in human relationships. Many of the stories entered this year, and several in this anthology, centre on isolation, perhaps because of the pandemic lockdowns the world is still experiencing. For readers now and in the future, it is vital to have writers create stories to reflect the time in which we live.

Particularly now, stories help us make connections. We are a community, those of us who write and read. This anthology makes a thought-provoking contribution to our community.

The judges thank Lucinda Sharp and Chris Champion for inviting us to participate in the Tasmanian Writers' Prize. It was a privilege to be the first outside readers of these stories and we felt a great responsibility as we debated our selections for the anthology. We mulled over the effectiveness of storylines, the quality of writing, the depth of characters and how each writer responded to the theme of island resonance. Congratulations to those writers whose stories you are about to read.

—*Penny Lane*

R.I. QUIN is a writer living and working from her home in regional Queensland. Her work is inspired by Outback landscapes and a love of solitude. Her short fiction has appeared in the Forty South Short Story Anthology 2020 *and in* Overland.

Saving Daniel

R.I. QUIN

The grass grew wild and wiry on the southern side of the island. Agnes waded through it, stepping cautiously on the rocky ground. She pulled her scarf across her face in an attempt to block out the blast of cold wind that blew up from the arctic mass sitting just below the horizon.

It was a lonely, solitary place, inaccessible by road and thought by most to be inaccessible by sea. At that time of year, and that time of day, no sun yet. A distant sketch of light in the east indicated the exact place at which the sun would rise, but mist and cloud cover made precise sunrises a rare thing. Most inhabitants of the island were still asleep or perhaps rising to sit in front of warm fires or cooked breakfasts. She knew the town, clustered in the north, gathered around the wide, expansive blue of the harbour, sheltered from the worst of the southerly winds, would be all but silent, all but still. Not to wake for another hour at least. By then she hoped to be back by her own fire.

She found her spot in a small alcove of rock in a place protected from the wind. She leant forward and peered out to the south.

Her heart was unsteady and her breathing rapid as her eyes traced lines across the wide, wild waters of the ocean. He would come. He would always come. But peering into the mist, watching, searching between fallen cloud and rising wave, there was always that moment when she believed in his absence with greater conviction than she believed in his ability to appear.

Then, at the moment when panic seemed ready to drown her, a small light would always shine through the dawn. First there, then gone an instant later. Blurred and imagined in mist. There again, and again. More there than not. The rest of the boat emerging to create substance for the light, and she smiled to herself, shook her head at her own disbelief.

The force of the wind crashed into her as she picked her way down the side of the island toward the rocks and the churning waves.

They played there as children: she, Lyle and Daniel. Other island children wandered the harbour's edge. They dodged in and out of coils of rope, tubs of salmon, crates of prawns, along the wharves. It was Daniel who loved the wild side of the island. He appeared at their door on the mornings they were free. Charmed their mother. Dragged them off. They followed him. Each step he took they followed. Each rock and crevice, each beating of wave on rock, each tidal pool, periwinkle, sea anemone — he knew them all, so she and Lyle knew them.

Still, she held her breath as the boat manoeuvred through the narrow gap between rocks, searching out the deep channel and settling with the swell into comfortable, calmer waters. The old smuggler's dock jutted out at a jagged angle, constructed around rock, moulded into the shape of the island so it couldn't be seen from the open ocean or from the cliffs above. The memory of it had been washed from the collective island psyche by storms and shipwrecks and the passing of the old seamen. Daniel had discovered it and restored it on those days when she and Lyle were caught up helping in the garden or with the firewood or out on the ocean in the fishing trawler. He had done it on his own, filling his empty hours, and Lyle had sulked because he wanted to be part of it; sulked until Daniel had shown them what it felt like to run wildly across the boards, fly off the end, legs tucked up tightly underneath them to splash into the icy ocean waters.

It was Daniel. He had shown them all this, and now she waited, with that small skerrick of doubt, at the end of the wharf. He was safe in the calm waters of the harbour, but she waited for him to pull up beside her, throw out the rope, jump from the deck, smiling, smelling of fish and diesel and ocean, and lift her up and swing her around, kiss her, own her.

"Be quick," he whispered in her ear. "They are like frightened mice, huddled together, half starved." He released her, grinning. "You will look after them. You always look after them." He bounded back onto the deck and into the cabin.

There were five, moving together like small parts of the one entity; swallows taking the same flight path, but without the sense of freedom swallows have. A grandmother, father, mother, two children, scarves wrapped tightly around their heads, covering their faces but not the fear in their eyes. So accustomed to fear, and when the door is left open, still huddled together unable to free themselves. The habit of fear clinging to them.

It was always the possessions they carried that moved Agnes. Not their faces, not their fear or the way they shuffled together. It was the way they clung to the small bundles of all the things they owned, as if letting go of them would untether them from some long-remembered happiness.

Agnes waited on the wharf till the boat cleared the narrow channel and once more entered the open ocean. She knew his course now. He would head out to sea, skirt around the bottom of the island in a wide arc. Enter the harbour from the north as if he'd come from the rich, warmer fishing grounds closer to the mainland.

They stood a little away from her, the small, huddled family. They were silent. Watched her. Waited for her.

Their patient acceptance annoyed her. She turned and began her ascent up the side of the island. She knew they followed, heard the shuffled, tentative footfall, the sound of rocks dislodged as they scrambled up the path that was so familiar, so easy for her. She waited for them, turned her eyes towards the ocean where the small speck of boat disappeared into the slow creeping dawn.

. . .

The cottage was low-set, dark stone crouching in the hollow as if ducking to avoid the force of the southerly wind. It sat close to the edge of the island, defying the scientific properties of balance, fixed to the rock as if growing from it. To Agnes it looked the most forlorn place in the world.

They stopped at the door, the small family pressing closer together, shrinking back from the bleakness of the stone building.

"It's okay," Agnes nodded and smiled. "It's nice inside."

When she opened the door, she released the memories of the place. Daniel's shelter from the anger of his father, from the cruelty of the other island children, from the fickle rages of the island's weather. She released the memories of the first time she and Daniel lay together. His arms gentle, their bodies close and warm.

She beckoned them in. The warmth from the fire, the smells of stew cooking on the stove, the comfortable furniture.

"There's food here." She opened the cupboard. "No power I'm afraid, but the wood box is full. I'll bring perishables, meat, milk, cheese, from the house as you need it. There are books, toys, spare blankets." She pulled open the door into another room. "The bedroom's in here with extra mattresses."

The tightness of their weave loosened. She noticed it as the realisation of the place began to take effect. The smallest boy stepped away. His father's hand immediately reached for him. It was a habit learnt over their long journey. The boy looked up at his father. The hand fell from his shoulder. He moved forward and crouched on the floor beside a small box of colourful plastic blocks.

"It's lonely out here," Agnes said. "It's very unusual for anyone to come this far south. Sometimes a boat will come in close to shore. Keep out of sight. Stay to the house during the day. We can't risk you being seen."

She stepped outside, closed the door on them, the quiet voice of the woman still hanging in the air. "Thank you," she had said.

But the word that settled in Agnes's mind was *risk*.

She felt nothing for them. Her heart was silent on the subject of the battered, scarred human beings she left in the middle of the floor in the warm, confined space inside the cottage. She never did feel anything for them. It was Daniel who felt everything. His heart, so connected to hers, held enough for both. She left hers unaffected, left it to concentrate on him, on the risks he took, on the fear she felt as a constant ache when he was away from her.

She turned her face towards the sea. There was a change in the feel of the air, in the strength of the wind. There would be a storm. She clenched her body tightly, walked quickly, the storm at her back, along the edge of the island, through the small forest of stunted pine and paper bark. Home.

...

"Lyle."

"Agnes."

His voice always sounded formal on the phone. His lawyer demeanour carrying over into every aspect of his life. He lived his profession, just as Daniel lived the ocean.

"It's done. They're here."

"Good. I'll organise the transfer as quickly as I can. No problems I hope?"

"No. All good." She tilted her head and listened to the increasing wind. "But there's a storm coming."

"Daniel still out?"

"He'll be in soon."

There was a silence between them. Ever since childhood their silences had been filled with things unsaid. That's how it was on the island, with the ocean surrounding them.

"Mum asked for you yesterday. You and Daniel. When this one's done, we'll have a break. Come over." He stopped. He laughed. "Come for a visit. Come. I can show you the sights. We can all be together."

"We'll see," she said. "Daniel won't ..."

"I'll talk to him."

. . .

The first time had been by chance. Daniel out on his own, fishing for mackerel and it was there, floundering in huge waves, a boat not fit to be out on the open ocean. He found two still alive. A woman clutching her silent, dead child. A man desperately trying to save them.

As Daniel approached, the boat disappeared below the waves, taking with it their possessions and the rest of their family. He pulled the two from the water, the woman still holding the child.

There had been a similar incident months before. Bill Grundy rescued a group of women and children, brought them back to the island. Daniel sat on the breakwater, elbows on his knees, and watched the police boat arrive to take them away.

"Treated them like criminals." He spat the words at Agnes. The words took away his smile, left him angry and ashamed. Agnes rubbed his shoulders, kissed the intensity of his brow. "Criminals," he repeated the word.

So he took the man and woman to the smugglers' cove. They wrapped the child in a blanket and buried him in a shallow grave beside the cottage.

He told Agnes.

He phoned Lyle.

He knew they couldn't save them all.

. . .

The storm grew.

Agnes glanced down into the hollow towards the cottage. They would be safe down there. Her resentment towards them was not personal. It was wrapped up with risk and the fear she felt. But they would be safe. They may be frightened by the storm, but they would be safe. For Daniel, she needed them to be safe.

Wind buffeted the car. Windscreen wipers flicked and swished, unable to keep up with the relentless rain. She pulled up in the car park beside the Fishing Co-op and scanned the harbour. Even within the safety of the harbour, the boats rocked precariously at their moorings, the wind rattled and smacked against the net riggings.

"Has he come in?"

She knew the answer to the question. Fredrick Hammel understood that she knew the answer. "I'll give him a call for you love." He reached across his desk. Took the hand set. The radio crackled. "Come in Daniel. Come in *White Gull*. Are you receiving?" His voice monotonous, giving away no emotion. He repeated the call.

"He should be in by now." Agnes leant forward.

"Probably holed up in some safe harbour over by Strandford of Billow. He received the storm warning last night."

"He should be back." She clenched her fist by her side. "He should be back."

"Look love," Fredrick patted her shoulder. He'd known her since she was a little, wild girl. He read the story of her loss in her eyes. She wore it there like all the fishermen's wives did. "I'll head out to the wharf, and down to the pub. Ask around. See if anyone caught sight of him out there."

. . .

The office felt small, smelt of damp and salt. She stood in the centre of it, her fists clenching and unclenching at her side.

Daniel knew of the storm. Knew of it and still brought them. Kept them safe. Thought of them, but didn't think of her. Didn't think of himself.

Hate and love require the same amount of passion. Anger and fear inhabit the same internal space.

The door flung open with the wind and storm. "No one's seen him love." Fredrick pushed his way into the office making the space smaller. "Can't send anyone out till the storm softens. You should go home, get some sleep."

He could see she was not going home.

"We'll go out first light. He'll be in some safe harbour, I'm sure of it. Your boy knows these waters better than most."

He's not in any safe harbour.

She wanted to shout the words. She wanted to reveal it all. Tell him she'd seen him at dawn on the other side of the island. Tell him Daniel was out there in the open water, trying to get back to her. Nothing else was important. She would risk it all for him to be back in the safety of the harbour.

Hot coffee in her hands, Fredrick persuaded her to sit on the office lounge. She looked out through the window to the harbour entrance. Waves rolled and crashed across the mouth, inundated the breakwater. It was impassable, she knew it was, but watched for him all the same.

. . .

The sea will take us all, her father had said. *In the end it will take us all.*

And it had taken him, deep, deep down. And the loss of him had swallowed her mother. The knowledge of him floating somewhere between the coral and the hump-backed swell of the ocean's surface had stolen the recognisable parts of her.

"I'll take her with me," Lyle said as they watched her.

She no longer looked at the ocean. She wandered along the beach, face towards the island, collected stones and saw only sand, hurled them at the waves, but looked skyward. Her lips moved constantly as she alternately cursed the sea and called her lost husband's name. Lyle took her to the mainland, to the city, where there was no view of the sea to remind her of loss and sadness. To the city where she returned to her painting and scenes of fishing boats safely moored in harbours, of calm summer days, sun glinting off the surface, waves trickling in to caress the sand.

"She'll be happier away from here," he said.

· · ·

Fredrick shook her arm. "We're heading out," he said, so close to her she felt the warmth of his breath.

She was awake in an instant, unaware she'd been asleep. She followed him out onto the wharf. His *Arabella*, lights on ready to push off. Three others on board, heads lowered, shoulders hunched, readying the boat. The sky was unusually clear, washed of storm, the last of the night stars beginning to fade with the first of the day's light.

"If he's out there," Fredrick called to her, "we'll find him for you."

She stood, looking out, watching the entrance of the harbour. The day began. The business of the wharf increased. The eyes of fishermen slid off her as they passed. Boats left the harbour, but none entered.

"Mrs." It was the young boy who manned the office when Fredrick was out. He stood close and repeated the word "Mrs."

She turned and looked at him.

"They've found him. Foundering all right. The engine's conked out, but he's fine. They're bringing him in."

She nodded.

. . .

At the top of the hill, she stopped the car. She saw them, the two boats strung together. The crippled vessel dragging out behind. He would come. He would always come.

But he would not see her like this.

She thought of the family in the cottage. He wanted to save them all. She only wanted to save him.

*HELEN WYATT lives in lutruwita (Tasmania). She writes poetry and prose —
for pleasure, for the challenge, and to try and make sense of life. Her short story,
"Maria Magic", was published in the* Forty South Short Story Anthology 2016.

Chasing the light

HELEN WYATT

She can drag herself no further. She lies down. She may never rise.

The pain in her leg is gone now. Blood no longer oozes from the gouges on her hands where she tried to catch the spindly shrubs as she tumbled over them. Or the jagged gash on the side of her head where she hit the cliff.

The earth pulls her close and her bones settle on the twigs beneath her. She feels her flesh loosen as if ready to slip into the wet, peaty soil.

Her thoughts are slippery and hard to grasp. In her head, her own voice seems to have drifted into the distance and become scrambled in the wind.

She shudders as a thousand regrets and a thousand sorrows billow, and then sighs as they settle like autumn leaves. The glow of a thousand joys warms her, and her ribs let her breathe again.

Her feet remember carrying her, sure and fast. Her body remembers lying with Adam, and the surge of bliss that he is her man. Her arms remember folding around Jesse as they placed him, wet and wonderful on her chest, and later the soft velvet of him as her lips kissed his fine downy hair — then his arms tight around her neck, her heart exploding. The miracle of holding him while he fed on that first morning, and looking out the window into the still, silver, predawn light. She had felt herself expanding — she and this babe, until they filled every corner of the world, every atom of the universe. She knew that she was now living a completely different life.

Her arms are warm with the memory of his weight, and she can feel a smile under the frozen skin of her face.

Her eyes remember weeping with love and with despair.

What power there is in loving. This child, this man, this life, this Earth. Her whole body is suddenly filled by the surging of her heart, and there is no room for her breath. She should have held them all closer; she should have listened more; she should have been braver; she should …

She coughs and her breathing steadies again.

Thoughts whisper through her mind, too feeble to grasp. Instead images flit behind her eyes. Jesse's face as he told her not to take this trip — what are you doing mum, you're an old woman now and you've been sick and if something happens you're on your own and you are so stubborn tell her dad.

Jessie. Strong, sure, and now a man. Always her child

And Adam's sigh. Hush Jesse. Your mother is prepared, she's done this a hundred times, and to more risky places. She'll set off her beacon if she runs into trouble, you know that. She needs to do this — it's what she fought for, lying in that hospital bed. His voice calm and confident and his eyes full of tenderness.

Oh, my loves …

Adam, who knows even the parts of herself she tries to hide; who knows this trip will make her whole again; who has faith in her; who she is letting down. He wanted to come with her, she could tell. But this she needed to do alone. To prove she can still do it. To dig out that person who had travelled to the isolated, craggy, challenging places. Those inhospitable, aloof places. Those intense places where the weather changes in a moment, placing you at the mercy of elemental forces that wrest control from your hands.

This journey had seemed a gentle one. Low risk and well thought out – but still it has been her undoing.

It was a perfect weather forecast – she would catch that tail of the storm time, when the sky is fractured, and the light is washed clean by the rain, and you never know quite what magic the lens might find. And it had all been there – they would find it in her camera. But not that last shot, where she leaned out to capture the dancing rainbows and droplets hanging like crystals in the air, while shafts of light burst from beyond the clouds like swords driven from the heavens into the grey green sea.

A signal of redemption.

A temptation. A prelude. An ending.

She imagines distant chatter – days away yet – of searching and panic and grief. Garbled voices – Adam and Jesse, trying to explain what has happened to her parents.

Oh God … her parents … they are so overjoyed at her recovery they want to shroud her in cotton wool. She didn't tell them about this trip. They'll blame her for being reckless. They won't understand. They never understand.

Their love was always a weight on her shoulders. From the very start they tried to make their choices her choices. At every crossroad they tried to steer her along a different path.

That's not a career for a girl!

You're married now, that's no career for a wife.

You're a mother now, you can't do that with a baby – take up portraiture instead.

You're sick, you'll have to put your camera aside now.

You've recovered now, but it may come back – you don't know how long you've got.

You don't know how long you're got . . .

But she was in the thrall of the light, and of all it touched. How could she turn away from the power, and the beauty, and the majesty, that the Earth revealed to her.

Voices woven with radio and telephone talk of routes, and planning and logistics, of maps and equipment and lists of volunteers, and urgency. But this is only day three. She will not be missed until day five when the dinghy returns for her.

She sees faces and calls to them *I'm sorry. I'm so sorry. I'd set off my beacon, but it's in my pack . . . lost . . . my arms are so weary. . .*

There is a tree above her that flicks at the sun shining weakly down on her face. She doesn't want to close her eyes, so she lowers her lids just enough to deflect the glare. The light will be gone soon enough.

Her bones creak. Her raincoat scrapes over the scratchy scoparia she lies on, protecting her from her bed's sharp leaves. A raven watches from high in a nearby tree. Fall . . . fall . . . *fall*, it mocks.

At the edge of her vision the mountain cliffs stand against the sky. Low clouds veil, and then reveal the escarpment in a dance as old as the rocks themselves.

She imagines herself rising to stand on the summit of the mountain. Her feet are wide and her legs stand strong. Her body expands with every breath, and she is weightless and free. She stands among clouds that are skittish and gusting, bunching and breaking, so that shafts of sun, and blotches of blue, churn with the mix of heavy, water laden grey, and bright glowing clumps of white. Below, a mosaic of green and grey lies, dapple draped over the earth's vast skeleton. Patches of vegetation and rock ripple together. Copses of gums are strewn across the landscape, and in the distance, stretches of button grass look like moss until, in every direction, the land meets the lace edged sea.

In her mind, her legs flex and she leans into the breeze that brushes her face. She closes her eyes and soars down the valley below. The wind rushes through her hair and she looks down at the creek snaking below her, shining silver under the sun and then vanishing momentarily into the shade of overhanging green.

And further, to rim of the island. The rocks on the shore which seem to shift with the mottled light, dressed in the weeds of the sea, warted with limpets and encrusted with clusters of tiny iridescent mussels – rocks dipping to be buried by golden sand. The waves pound at the rocks as if trying to drag them into the depths, and foam lies in drifts across the beach. The water surges and breaks against the cliffs, and then pulls back as the unending swell heaves across the ocean from the south.

...

The never-resting waters of the straight had been gentle when she came here, dabbling among the rocks and murmuring over the sand, flicking spray playfully at the feet of the cliffs beyond the rocks.

Just days ago she waded onto that beach with her boots tied around her neck and her pack held above her head. Her shoulders had ached from the strain, and her legs had ached from the icy water, but she had felt like a hero embarking on a quest, a conqueror returning in victory to her birthplace. As the dinghy powered from the island she had turned and watched the churn of foam as it shrank from view. She had listened as the drone of the outboard motor was swallowed by the song of the lapping waves and the calling gulls.

Now, below, she sees herself; leg askew, lying amid pineapple grass and bauera, and suddenly there is sleet and mist, and she falls back into her body.

This body that has carried her across mountain ranges and chasms, across oceans and deserts in search of a lifetime of illusive images. This body that has given and received such tenderness of touch that it has melted, again and again. This body that has carried and delivered a life so precious and beautiful that it forever seems magical. And this body that had fought the cancer that tried to destroy it. This body that has brought her here and has given her this final gift.

Because instantly she knows. Everything must pass, and this is her time. Not isolated in a hospital bed, an island linked by tubes and monitors in a sea of machinery metal and plastic, amid beeps and whirrs, the antiseptic scent of death — and artificial light unending, unchanging. Tethered only by Adam's warm hand holding hers, across an alien, terrifying abyss.

She had fought, draped by that white sheet … willing herself not to die under those spiritless lights.

The cold cradles her as the sun dips lower in the sky. Golden rays brush the rocks above, niggling into crevices and tangling with the straggled vegetation clinging there, only to be swept away again by the scudding clouds in a never-ending, ever changing masterpiece. This is the light that will carry her, as it always has. This light, coming from the stars will be with her as her spirit flies, and her body, this small collection of atoms that has come together for a only a moment, begins its journey to rejoin the universe.

Specks of sleet tickle her eyelashes and her eyelids twitch. Tiny flakes rest on her lips, and she parts them to let the drops trickle into her mouth.

She is not a woman dying in a cage.

She is a woman chasing the light.

She is the light.

LEAH CARTER decided to try her hand at fiction after years of corporate writing. Not one to do things by halves, she wrote two novels at the same time and hopes to see them both in print. Now she wants to add short story writing to her list of things to conquer. Leah lives in Tauranga, New Zealand but still dreams of Tasmania after a long holiday there many years ago.

Roadkill

LEAH CARTER

"Welcome to tiger country, son."

Dad beamed as he clutched the steering wheel, his unruly hair swirling in the breeze. "Smell that fresh air."

He pointed in various directions. "Would you look at those mountains." Then, seconds later, "That's the most gorgeous view I've ever seen."

Suddenly the car lurched to the left, catching me off guard. "Jeez, Dad. Maybe you should focus on keeping the car on the road."

"Might take a while to get used to driving on this side. Feels very strange. But it's all part of the adventure, isn't it son?"

"Mmm."

The only reason I'd agreed to go on this trip was because Mom guilt-tripped me. Went on and on about how miserable Dad had been since the divorce. It was alright for *her*. She had a new husband and a baby on the way. But not Dad. He hadn't bounced back like she said he would. According to Mom, organising this little surprise for my 13th birthday had made him happier than he'd been in ages. Give it a chance, she'd pleaded.

But it turned out it wasn't a *little* birthday surprise. Flying more than 17,000 kilometres across the Pacific Ocean to an Australian island I'd never heard of was *huge*.

"Why Tasmania?" I'd asked when he showed me on Google maps. "Why so far away? Surely we can find an island to explore closer to home. I don't see why we have to go to the end of the flippin' earth."

Dad tried to hide the hurt on his face. "It's just … I thought …" He covered his eyes with his hands and my heart lurched.

"So, what's it like then, Dad? This island?"

He took a couple of minutes to piece himself together, then quietly described some of Tasmania's attractions: the pristine wilderness, ancient forests, something different and new. By the end, he sounded like a travel agent. So much of me wanted to escape to my every-second-weekend room, grab my controller and lose myself in my preferred reality. But his desperate eyes made me stay put and listen.

"There's something else that's special about Tasmania, or Tassie like they call it in Australia."

"What's that, Dad?" I asked, glancing at the clock.

"They have tigers there. Tasmanian tigers."

My face must have given it away. He knew he'd gotten a bite. A big one.

"Really? Tigers?"

I'd always had a soft spot for cats, especially big scary ones. I still carted one of my toy tigers back and forth from Mom's house to Dad's. I found it hard to let them go.

"Tasmania is famous for them."

I eyed him suspiciously. "I've never heard that before."

"You said you'd never even heard of Tasmania before." He paused. "We could look for one in the wild. Imagine that! What do you say, Riley?"

Even though I knew this trip was more about him than me, I found myself nodding. "Okay then, Dad. Let's do it."

And here we were. Speeding along a road in the middle of nowhere on our tiger hunting adventure. Glancing around at the strange land, it felt like we were in a post-apocalyptic world. Every now and then another car would zoom past but aside from that, it was us and the wilderness.

I was about to ask him about the wifi at the lodge when the car came to a screeching halt.

"What the hell is *that?*" Dad said, stopping in the middle of the road. Peering over the hood, I could see a big brown lump directly in front of us. It was an animal of some kind. Medium-sized, like a small bear. It lay still, lifeless.

Dad carefully manoeuvred the car around it, then parked to the side of the road. "I'm gonna have a look at it."

He flung open the door and walked tentatively toward it. I found myself a few steps behind him.

"Well, it's not a tiger, that's for sure."

The creature was lying on its back with its four paws in the air.

"It looks like a brown pig." My eyes refused to look away. "It's so weird. What is it, Dad?"

"Looks a bit like a gopher, but bigger. Poor thing. Must have been hit by a car."

I turned to get back into the rental.

"I think we should move it off the road," Dad said. "Could cause an accident."

"What do you mean by *we*," I said, grimacing. "I'm not touching that. It's gross."

"Come on, Riley. We can't leave it here. How about you grab its back legs and I'll take the front."

I shook my head like he was offering me tofu. "Absolutely not." But Dad was already in position. I huffed, walked over to the icky beast and hastily dragged it into the nearby grass. I couldn't look at it. I forced my eyes onto my shoes and kept them there the whole time.

Back in the car, Dad patted my leg. "Proud of you, son."

I rubbed my hands with sanitiser. "I'm *never* doing that again."

As we drove, we saw a steady stream of roadkill. At first, we pointed them out to one another. But after a while we passed them in silence. Little bodies, bigger bodies, most of them unidentifiable aside from the rabbits. Still, no dead tigers, so at least that was something.

But as sunset approached, something changed. The Tasmanian wilderness came alive. Out of nowhere, kangaroos bounced across the road. We'd notice funny-looking hedgehogs creeping along. Or we'd catch a glimpse of a black dog-like critter making a run for it. We had to slow to a crawl to get to where we were headed because Dad was so worried about hitting something. Roadlife, Dad called it. He was buzzing, enthralled by everything around him.

I was yawning non-stop by the time we finally pulled into the lodge car park. It was like an oasis in a desert. A giant log cabin perched in the middle of a forest. With its warm lights glowing, it looked welcoming and homely.

"What do you think, Riley?" Dad said, smiling.

I gave him a thumbs up.

It didn't take us long to haul our bags from the car and settle into our room. My stomach was rumbling by the time we wandered down to the restaurant. It was crowded; it felt strange to see so many people, after seeing so few on the journey.

We were halfway through our meal when Dad mentioned our plan for the next day. We would hike along a trail near the lodge. He reverted to his travel agent speak when he told me about the treasure trove of natural wonders that surrounded us. I couldn't help but smile. It was the happiest I'd seen him in a long time.

"What about the tigers, Dad? Do you reckon we'll see one tomorrow?"

"Sure thing. Can't see why not." He guzzled his wine and sat back in his chair. "This is the life, isn't it?"

A waiter appeared out of nowhere and began filling his glass.

"So do they look the same as normal tigers? With orange stripes?" I asked.

I assumed Dad hadn't heard me because he didn't answer straight away. "Dad? The Tasmanian tigers?"

The waiter nodded politely at Dad, then looked straight at me.

"Are you on the hunt for a Tasmanian tiger?" he said, then shot Dad a look. "I hate to tell you both this, but ..."

"Hey!" Dad interrupted. "He was pointing excitedly at something out the window. I think I saw one of those tiny kangaroos bounce right past."

"Wallabies," the waiter corrected. "They're wallabies. There's heaps around here. If you go outside with a torch later on, you'll be sure to see lots of wildlife. This place is teeming with it."

"That's a splendid idea. Thanks, um, Greg," said Dad, reading his name badge.

"Though you're not going to see any ..."

"And another one!" said Dad, bouncing around on his chair. "Two in less than a minute. Amazing!"

I couldn't resist. I found myself squinting out the window, searching too. "I think I saw something in the bushes over there. Did you see it, Dad?"

I was so caught up in the moment, I didn't notice the waiter slip away.

. . .

At dawn, I was woken by a deafening beep-beep-beep next to my ear. I wearily tumbled out of bed and threw on some clothes since I knew Dad was keen to get going early. He was already up making breakfast. I wolfed down the cereal, threw some warm gear into my backpack, then we headed out the door.

The well-marked track was off to the right of the lodge. As we walked to the start point, Dad chatted non-stop about what we'd see in the day ahead of us. Giant trees, a magical rainforest and awe-inspiring glimpses of the valley and mountain. It was like my down-trodden dad had been replaced with this upbeat one. He'd even brushed his hair that morning *and* shaved.

It took us about an hour before we came across others on the track. It was a family with two children — a boy about my age and a young girl maybe six or seven years old. They were sitting on a rock to the side of the track nibbling on some snacks.

"That was *my* one," the girl yelled. "Give it back!"

"Shhh," the mom said. "I think I heard something."

As Dad and I drew closer, we stopped mid-step. We had both heard it, the sound of a branch breaking and the rustle of leaves. There was something in the forest.

I leaned over and whispered to Dad. "Maybe it's a tiger." He put his finger up to his mouth, indicating for me to be quiet.

"It might be a wombat," said the mom quietly. She looked over at us and smiled. "Just stay still and keep your eyes open."

I stood like a statue, except for my eyes which were darting about. I could see the little girl was already bored because she started fiddling with her shoelaces.

"There!" whispered the boy. "It's there."

He was pointing off to our right-hand side, toward a dense patch of bush. A short, stocky bear emerged and wandered across the path on all fours. It plodded along, completely disinterested in us. I immediately recognised it as the same creature we had seen dead on the road. It was the most curious looking animal I had ever seen. Its big round face, sturdy build and short legs. I couldn't take my eyes off it.

"Wombat!" said the little girl. "It's a wombat."

The wombat looked up, startled by the noise, then darted off at a surprisingly fast speed. We all stared after it.

The dad was first to break the silence. "Is that the first time you've seen a wombat?" he asked us.

"It's the first living one we've seen," said Dad. "We saw one on the road yesterday. Must have been hit by a car. I had no idea what it was. Thought it was a small bear. A wombat, you say. Amazing."

He was shaking his head in wonder like he'd just seen a unicorn. I shrugged at the boy. He shrugged back. Dad started chatting to the kids' parents so I left him and started ambling along the track. The boy followed me. I could still hear Dad babbling on about the island's incredible scenery and rich landscape. He was doing his travel agent thing again.

"Hey," said the boy as he sidled up to me.

"Hey," I said back.

"I heard what you said before."

I must have given him a blank stare because then he said, "About the tiger."

I shrugged again. "What about it?"

He kicked a stone into the bushes and the noise made the girl yell out.

"Wombat?" she called out, her golden pig-tails swaying back and forth as she looked all around.

The boy kicked another stone. The girl huffed loudly and went back to her shoelaces.

"Are you looking for one? A Tasmanian tiger?"

It took me a minute to understand his funny twang. "Yeah," I said nodding. "We came to Tasmania to see one in the wild."

The boy studied my face, like he was searching for the answer to a question. I wondered if he was a bit weird.

"Well, you won't find one," he said, finally.

I scrunched up my face. "Why not?"

I couldn't work out if he was trying to annoy me or if he was being serious.

"Because they are extinct. There haven't been any Tasmanian tigers for almost a hundred years."

. . .

I stomped through the bush with the wrath of a stroppy toddler. I could tell it was bothering Dad because he wasn't talking as much. He'd tried to start up a few conversations after the wombat sighting, but I didn't bite.

"You seem a bit upset, Riley. Something up?"

Yes, something was up. I'd been brought halfway round the world to look for something that didn't exist! All this time he had me thinking I was going to see a tiger. And I believed him. It was all a lie. The whole trip. A big fat lie. How could I have been so stupid? Of course there weren't tigers here. Had I really been so dumb to think they would be roaming around?

I kept stomping, my mouth firmly closed.

"Alright then. But if you want to talk about it, you know you can tell me anything."

There was something I definitely wanted to tell him. That this was the worst birthday present ever. But instead I fumed and stormed on.

. . .

We were sitting on the sofa next to the gigantic fireplace in the corner of the restaurant. The crackle of the fire, the soft music, the hum of chatter around us was making it difficult for me to stay angry. Plus I was exhausted from all that walking.

Dad was gibbering about the day. The magic of this place. The incredible beauty of everything. The awe-inspiring wildlife. Perhaps he thought if he talked enough, I'd eventually talk back. He was throwing out words like "revitalised" and "energised" like he was in an energy-drink commercial. And that's when I realised how different he looked. He was animated, throwing his arms around. His eyes were full of expression.

I tuned into what he was saying. He said the change in scene had made him see everything differently. That maybe it was time for him to try something new. Perhaps look for another job. Or maybe he could go back to college and study. He said it was something he'd always wanted to do.

"There are so many possibilities, even for an old guy like me."

Drawn into his energy, I looked up at him and smiled. "Good for you, Dad. That's great."

And the thing was, I meant it.

His smile disappeared and his face crumpled. He threw his arms around me and squeezed tight. I didn't fight it.

We stayed like that for a few minutes. I wasn't sure if it was the flames or my dad's arms that warmed me inside.

Finally, he let go. "How about we have another go looking for that Tasmanian tiger tomorrow?"

I waited for the sparks to catch, but there was nothing.

Instead, I nodded. "Sure thing, Dad."

GAIL CHRISFIELD lives and works on unceded Wadawurrung Country on Victoria's Surf Coast. Her short fiction has been published by Margaret River Press. Her voluntary roles include Regional Ambassador for Writers Victoria, Coordinator of Words from the Surf Coast Arts Trail and Convenor of Write Here in Surf Coast.

Butterfly girl

GAIL CHRISFIELD

The rain stops as I veer off the road and brake. For a moment, I think I'm in the wrong place. The twisted moonah tree in the distance assures me I'm not.

The asphalt and white paint, timber bollards and rails weren't here last time. Neither were the yellow and red-lidded bins. But the view down the hill to where the cliff ends and the ocean begins is the same. The tangle of moonahs and other melaleuca species to the right, eucalypts and wattles to the left.

"Here we are, baby girl," I whisper.

I steer the car into a rectangular parking bay. Reverse and edge forward to fit more evenly between the lines.

"We didn't have to do this last time, did we, Eloise?" A quiet laugh escapes my lips. "Silly Mummy. There's nobody else here to worry about."

There was no one around that day either. Not until later.

I nudge the bumper bar against the rail, cut the engine. The windscreen wipers continue to whump left to right, right to left. I flick them off and sit in the silence. Peer over the bonnet to where we parked the last time we came to the island. The twisted moonah tree halfway down the hill.

Without warning, my heart takes off like it wants to jump out of my chest. I unbuckle my seat belt, lean back, close my eyes. Rest my hands on my diaphragm and take in one long, slow breath followed by a longer, slower exhalation.

I hear my counsellor's voice in my head. "In, one, two, three, four. Out, one, two, three, four, five, six, seven, eight. In, one, two, three, four ..."

When I've gone through the sequence enough times to calm the pounding in my chest, I open my eyes and sit up. Open the door and get out of the car. The icy wind blowing in off the strait lashes my face, making my nose run and my eyes water. I swipe my cheeks with the back of my hand.

The sealed car park and its bin collection aren't the only changes. The sign with an arrow pointing down the hill is new too. I walk across to read what it says.

My breath seizes. For a second I'm not sure I'll ever be able to breathe again. I'm saved by a small sob escaping my lungs.

I fumble in my pockets for a handkerchief or a tissue. Empty. I swear under my breath. Stumble back to the car and open the door.

. . .

As soon as I unbuckle her seat belt, Eloise springs from her booster seat like a jack-in-the-box. Pushes past me, jumps out of the car and skips away.

"Hey, slow down, baby girl," I say.

She keeps going, ponytails bouncing, wisps of dust at her feet.

"Stop, Eloise." I sprint after her.

She pulls up beside the worn timber steps at the top of the cliff. Throws out her arms.

"Look, Mummy, look." She turns, her face the same picture of wonder as on Christmas morning. "Look at all the water."

I go to grab her. She spins out of my reach.

"I can see the sea, I can see the sea," she sings.

Her light summer dress balloons from its bodice. She looks like the spinning top her grandpa has made for her fourth birthday. Only nine sleeps to go.

She stops and teeters into me. "Oh, Mummy, I'm so izzy-whizzy."

I enfold her in my arms. Gaze across the wide expanse of ocean to where it meets the sky. Somewhere beyond there is the mainland and the home my husband and I built together before our daughter was born.

The water sparkles like a gazillion diamonds. Warm air brushes my skin, the tang of eucalypt and salt grazes my nostrils. A symphony of bird song fills my ears; seagulls of course, but also kookaburras and other native residents of the garden we're here to visit.

I pick out the "Woooo-wit-woo. Woooo-wit-woo" of one I recognise.

"Hear that, Eloise? It's a willy wagtail singing."

She turns to face me, blue eyes wide. "What's a silly wagtail?"

"A cheeky little bird that's always on the move, just like you." I tickle her.

Eloise's laugh tinkles. She pushes away from me. Flaps her arms and chirps, "I can fly. I can. Look, Mummy. I'm a silly wagtail."

"Of course you are."

A flash of orange and black flits by. I turn. Glimpse the pair of tiny wings flickering in the sunlight before they disappear into the shady garden.

I point after them. "Let's check out what's over there."

Eloise pauses her bird dance, arms suspended mid-air. "Why?"

"Maybe we'll find some butterflies."

"Flutterbyes." She claps her hands and skips along the clifftop.

"Wait."

I catch up with her. Wrap my fingers around her tiny hand. Fondle its moist warmth. Rummage in my pocket for my phone. Swear under my breath.

"Eloise, sweetie. We have to go back to the car for a minute."

"Why?"

"Because I left my phone there."

Eloise pouts, wriggles her hand out of mine. "I don't want to go back to the car. I want to see the flutterbyes."

"Car first, then flutterbyes, okay? And whoever gets to the car first gets a surprise."

Eloise swings her head towards the car, the garden, the car. She laughs and takes off. "Run, run, run as fast as you can. You can't catch me, I'm the Gingerbread Man."

I wait until she's halfway. Chase after her.

"I won," she says as I get to the car. She falls against me, out of breath.

"Yes, you did." I bend down, heft her up on to my hip. "Ouff. You're growing up way too fast. Mummy won't be able to do this much longer."

She wraps her arms around my neck, smooches my cheek. "Where's my surprise?"

"It's coming." I plant a kiss on her forehead. Grapple with the door handle.

. . .

Tugging a wad of tissues from the box in the console, I wipe my eyes, blow my nose. Dump the squidgy mass into the cup holder.

I lean over to lift my coat off the back seat. My hand brushes the patch of dark fabric where Eloise's booster seat used to be — before her father removed it.

"Bastard," I whisper. "You didn't even ask. Just went ahead and did."

I pull my coat through the gap between the two front seats. Wrap it around me, cram phone and tissues into its pockets. Stretch across to pick up the posy of native flowers occupying the front passenger seat.

Two wire butterflies — one coated in pink glitter, the other in silver — poke out from the middle of the arrangement. As I close the door and lock the car, they flap in the wind. The florist meant well, but I didn't order these tawdry additions. I yank them out, march over to the bins, toss them in.

I pass between two bollards and head down the hill, taking care not to slip. At the twisted moonah tree I pause. This is where I parked that day. It was dusty dry earth and gravel then. Today it's verdant with native grasses.

Out of nowhere, an invisible fist punches me in the chest. I double over, breathless. Drop the flowers, suck in air.

"Eloise, my baby girl, my baby girl." My voice is swamped by the rumble of the waves breaking against the cliffs.

I've held off coming back here for so long; 12 months, two years. Last week when the borders reopened; I agreed with my counsellor it was time.

Now I'm here, drowning. It's agony but I let it happen, go with it. Surrender.

When I surface, I dry my eyes, retrieve the flowers. Take a deep breath, relax my shoulders and walk past the twisted moonah tree.

"I'm coming, baby girl. I'm coming."

. . .

Eloise runs ahead of me, disappears into the garden through a gap between the eucalypts and wattles.

I wipe my sweaty face with the back of my hand. "Hey, wait for me."

"Hurry up, Mummy."

"I'm coming."

At the entrance, I pause. Eloise is darting around the garden after butterflies. "Oooh," she trills.

She jumps, swings her hands through the air to catch one. Misses.

I walk towards a wooden bench under a tree. Hold up my phone. "Hey, Butterfly Girl."

She stops. "Look at all the pretty flutterbyes. There's so many."

"Smile and let Mummy take a photo."

"No." She laughs and chases after another butterfly.

"C'mon."

I have her in frame, almost in focus. She changes direction and dashes off again. "You can't catch me. You can't catch me."

A message pops up on my screen. *Battery critically low. Connect to recharge now.*

Annoyed at myself for not putting the phone on recharge in the car, I'm about to give up and switch it off. Eloise appears on screen.

She's as still as a statue, riveted by something in the palm of her hand. At first, I think it's a flower, until the camera picks up the quiver of delicate wings. They remind me of her soft lashes brushing my cheek with a butterfly kiss.

"Beautiful," I whisper.

I take the photo. Sit on the bench and tap into the image gallery. Thumbnails dawdle onto screen one-by-one. The newest comes up last. I click on it. The screen turns black.

The crunch of tyres skidding through gravel. I look up. Where's Eloise?

...

I race through the gap between eucalypts and wattles. Stop. "There you are," I say.

Eloise and her butterfly are standing near the wooden bench. My head spins. I don't know whether to laugh or cry.

I stagger across to the bench, flop down like a rag doll. Rest my head on my knees. Listen to my breath, in and out, like the ebb and flow of the waves on the shore.

After several minutes, I sit up and salvage my phone from the depths of my coat pocket. Bring up the photo I took that day. Compare it to the life-size bronze sculpture before me.

The artist has done an amazing job. The likeness between photo and statue is striking. Both capture the moment between Eloise and the butterfly, each transfixed by the other.

The moment before the butterfly flew off and Eloise ran after it. Before the swoosh and the woman screaming. Before the paramedics and the police officers. The journalists and photographers. The sympathetic islanders, here from the start, keen to help.

Before all the curious mainlanders who came later, lured by the Facebook page and crowdfunding campaign set up by Eloise's father. They're long gone now, back to the mainland taking him with them. The butterflies have gone too. But I've come back to stay.

I stand and approach the statue. "Hey, baby girl, Mummy's here."

I wipe raindrops from Eloise's face. Step back. Set my flowers on the ground beside the plaque. Reach into my pocket for tissues. Bend down to clean the muck away from the inscription. Read the words.

Butterfly Girl
In memory of Eloise Joy

I breath out a long sigh. Straighten up, find my phone, take a photo. "Oh, Eloise. I miss you so much, baby girl."

I close my eyes, bow my head. Stand in the silence. Breathing. Present.

"Woooo-wit-woo. Woooo-wit-woo"

The bird's song brings me out of myself. I open my eyes. The winter sun has broken through the gunmetal clouds and the hint of a rainbow arcs over Eloise's bronze head.

"Beautiful."

I lean in to kiss her brow. A soft flutter skims my cheek, like the memory of a butterfly kiss. I smile. The butterflies will be back in the spring.

TAMARA HAJDU is an aspiring writer. She currently works at Gold Coast Libraries and studies creative writing in her spare time. She was living on the Southern Moreton Bay Islands when the first murder (since white settlement in 1834) was recorded there. It remains unsolved.

The likeness

TAMARA HAJDU

In the mornings Susan potters in her front garden, pulling non-existent weeds, hoping for mail and the excuse to have a chat with Paul, the island postie. On the days that he speeds past, a cloud of dust in his wake, she feels a pang of disappointment. Of course, he can't always stop. Paul has a wife and two boys at home, not to mention how busy he is going to the Johnson woman's house every day, helping her out with the things she needs. Or needed, rather. It's hard to believe, what they say he's done.

Susan pores over the papers that Rob and Jan have brought over. She didn't know the Johnson woman personally, only Paul. Inside Susan's house, Rob fiddles with cords at the back of the television, presses buttons on the remote. Jan and Susan sit on the veranda, talking, trying to fill in the gaps. *Barb says she seen him at the RSL for weeks, playing the pokies with great wads of cash,* says Jan. She knows everyone in the community, bar the newcomers. *Everyone knew that Marg kept large amounts of money at home. Meanwhile where's Paul getting all that dough when he's only working 3 hours a day delivering mail?* Susan wants to disagree, to defend Paul, but this last fact hangs there in the air between the two women, heavy with meaning.

The wind picks up, and Susan hastily puts her hand on the paper, weighing down the fluttering edges with objects close to hand; the rusted mozzie coil holder, her heavy ceramic mug, the ashtray she bought for when Jan visits. Susan points to something on the page. *Why don't they say how Margaret Johnson died? They just say it was –* Susan runs her finger down the page, finds the quote she is searching for – *violent and unnatural. Oh!* says Jan. Another fact she hasn't told Susan. *They reckon she got her head bashed in with a hammer or some such thing,* she says. Susan looks up from the paper in shock.

Sooner they bloody well arrest him the better, yells Rob from inside the house.

He slides the screen door open, joins the women on the veranda. *That telly's toast,* he tells them. Susan looks dismayed. *But I've missed almost a week of my shows,* she says. What Susan doesn't say is that she has missed all the news reports on the Johnson murder. She wants to keep this hidden; someone's death isn't entertainment. So why can't she stop thinking about what has happened?

Jan points at a glossy catalogue on the coffee table that has come with the papers. *Why don't you pick a new television from there? Rob can bring it over for you, he's going to the mainland on Thursday.* Rob and Susan immediately protest but Jan forcefully crushes their objections. *People take much bigger things than a television on the boat,* she tells them with an air of finality, *and if buying a new television is inevitable, you may as well do it sooner rather than later.* Susan blinks in surprise.

After some hasty deliberation — it's all happening so quickly! — Susan selects a television from the catalogue, circles it in a felt tip pen. Susan sheepishly hands Rob the catalogue, gives him a look intended to convey, *are you sure you don't mind?* Rob gives Susan a faintly perceptible nod and Susan feels more at ease.

Susan excuses herself and goes to her bedroom, slides open the bedside drawer, opens a bulging envelope, retrieves five $100 notes. She licks her forefinger to wet it and counts through the bundle, double and triple checking the amount. When she's satisfied, Susan goes back outside and holds it out to Rob. *$500. For the television.* There's a beat, and then Rob takes the money with a quiet nod, eases it into one of his pockets. There's a silence, and Susan feels the need to say something more. *It goes without saying, but keep the change for the trouble,* she adds. Jan, who has been watching the whole exchange, waves the offer away as she answers for her husband. *It's no trouble, is it darl?*

Rob sighs loudly, stands up silently and heads back inside. Susan hears clattering and the sound of water; Rob at the kitchen sink, washing his mug. She wonders if he's upset, and catches Jan's eye. Jan shakes her head and silently mouths, *Don't worry, he's fine.* There are more noises from inside. A short time later, Rob emerges from the living room, carrying the old television, heading in the direction of his car. The two women exchange a confused look. *To take to the tip,* Rob explains. His mood is even-tempered, amiable. The women pause a moment, and watch him maneuver the load into the trunk with care. Jan turns to Susan. *Ah, Rob thinks of everything,* she says with pride. *Don't you worry about that.*

· · ·

Several days pass until Rob returns with Susan's new television. As Rob lugs the box into her living room, Susan hovers around awkwardly. Rob doesn't normally visit without Jan. It's the two women who are friends; Rob just tags along, helping Susan around the house with things that need doing. Rob lays the box down carefully on Susan's living room rug, and sets to unboxing and setting it up for her. Susan is apologetic, asking too many times, *are you sure you don't mind?* Rob insists that it's fine. *Jan's been bossing me about 40-something years. You'd better believe that I'm used to it by now.* They both smile. Susan concedes that Jan does have a strong personality. Their eyes meet - discussing Jan in her absence shifts the dynamic. Rob makes a joke — *it better not be a bloody fridge you need next time!* and Susan laughs and stops asking. Slowly the words begin to flow more easily.

Switching on the new television, the screen is a blur of static. It's dark now, and Susan turns on the lights, busies herself in the kitchen, as Rob attempts to coax it to pick up reception. When Susan returns, Rob proudly shows off the results; Gold Coast and Brissy stations! Susan is thrilled. Satisfied with his labours, Rob hands Susan the remote, eases onto the sofa, picks up his tea that she's prepared for him. As she flicks through the channels, Rob starts speaking - *there's one last thing* — but hesitates. Susan mutes the television and turns to him. *Tell me*, she says. Rob appears to be embarrassed. Susan waits. Before she retired she was a psychologist; she knows how to stretch out a silence. *The price of the television was $100 more than in the catalogue*, Rob says, looking away. *I covered it for you though.*

Susan clasps her hand to her mouth. How could she make a mistake like this? The catalogue must have been out of date. Immediately Susan goes to her bedroom to retrieve enough to cover the shortfall. Rob calls out, reassures her that he doesn't need it straight away, but Susan insists, returns to the living room, holds the green $100 note out to him. He hesitates, then reaches for it.

This is when it begins. For the brief moment that they are both touching the note Susan feels an odd sensation. An undercurrent of resistance, of wanting to refuse. It feels as though power is shifting. Susan pushes it away, and the moment passes. Rob thanks her, finishes his tea, chats for another ten minutes — she doesn't remember what about, it was ordinary, mundane — before heading home to Jan. It would only be later that she'd remember this moment as important.

Later that night as Susan is flattening the mountain of cardboard packaging in her living room she notices something odd. The glossy cardboard packaging has a bare patch where the barcode is, as though a sticker or price tag has been torn off. Susan stops. *Did Rob lie about the cost?* she thinks. Immediately Susan reprimands herself. All this thought about the Johnson woman is making her paranoid. What is she going to do, demand the receipt from him? Ring the store to confirm the price? She can trust Rob. She's not going to let her imagination get the better of her. In the end Susan decides she's being silly, resolves to forget about it.

Over the next few days, Susan sits intently in front of the television during the nightly news reports, her thumb hovering over the red record button. She enjoys the experience of rewinding the tapes, rewatching them, familiarising herself with the cast: the coppers brought over from the mainland, the dog walker who found the hammer in the mangroves, the clip of Paul that they play over and over, *It was only Sunday that I saw her. Everything was fine . . . normal.* Susan notices how tired Paul looks, how stressed. She hasn't seen him since all this happened. They've replaced him on the mail run for now.

Jan is a better source than the newspaper and television combined. When Susan's phone rings one morning, Jan is breathless with news. *Beryl who lives across from Paul and Donna. She's seen the coppers parked outside all morning, taking things from the house.* Susan is suddenly alert. Together the two women speculate. The police must be searching Paul's house, trying to find evidence. *Paul would be bloody ropable now, knowing him,* says Jan. As they talk, there are two beeps in the background. *Got another call. I'll ring you back,* says Jan, hanging up abruptly. Susan doesn't mind; there'll be new nuggets of information when she does call back. Susan sinks into the chair at the kitchen table to wait. She flips idly through the paper when something on the buy/swap/sell page catches her eye. A photo of a television, the same brand as her old one, *Works well, $300 ono, call Rob.*

Susan breathes in sharply. Puts on the cheap glasses she got from the chemist, squints closely at the blurry photo. In an instant Susan knows. This is hers. A wave of righteous anger rises inside of her. Furiously, she retrieves her battered address book, turns to the page with Rob's mobile number. Susan cross checks it with the number in the paper. It doesn't match. Susan feels deflated, doesn't know what to think. The television looks like her old one but it is possible that it's not. She cuts out the ad, glues it to the back page of her scrapbook. Stares at it. Later when Susan tells her son about it, he laughs, much to her irritation. Mum, it's just a coincidence. Televisions all look the same. You said yourself the phone number isn't his. The island is a small place. Don't go ringing and bothering randoms over this. She finds herself irritated with him, cuts him off. *Are the grandkids there? Put them on.*

. . .

Several days pass until Rob and Judy visit again. Uncharacteristically, Susan walks all the way out to their car parked on the verge to meet them. When Rob pops open the boot, Susan glances inside. Other than Jan's walking frame, the trunk is empty, save for a blanket lining the boot and a few green bags. The television is gone.

Taken the telly to the tip already? Susan tries to sound casual. *Yep, done it last Tuesday.* Susan feels her hackles rise when he says this. She is convinced that he's lying. *New one good?* Rob asks. He's focused on unfolding Jan's walking frame but when she doesn't answer he stops, looks up at her. Susan holds eye contact with him a moment too long, searching for signs of insincerity. She remembers that he asked her a question. *Yeah. It's good,* she says distractedly. Rob looks at her strangely.

Today when Susan and Jan settle down on the veranda, Susan struggles to pay attention to Jan. She can see Rob through the veranda window, opening and closing cupboards, moving around inside her house, going about his business. For the first time Susan notices that he's as comfortable there as if it was his own home. A sense of unease comes over her. She doesn't want him alone in her house anymore. Where is he poking around, while she and Jan are occupied outside? ... *I'll do it, next time I go to the Royal Brissy,* she hears Jan say. Susan forces herself to look away, refocuses her attention on Jan. *Oh. Maybe. I'll think about it.*

Later that night, as Susan draws her curtains, she sees the light of Rob and Jan's house, faintly through the thick bushland. Susan tries not to think about the money she keeps in her bedroom drawer, and other places too. Not to think about the Johnson woman, bashed multiple times with a blunt object in her own home. Not to think about who she can trust.

. . .

Over the next few weeks, more details emerge. The owners of the hammer have been found. An island couple have seen the photos of the battered hammer, laid out next to a ruler and photographed from different angles, and come forward. It had the Johnson woman's DNA on it. *We lent it to Paul a few years ago,* they say. *He never gave it back.*

The next morning, Rob and Jan show up unannounced. Jan is talking so fast Susan can barely understand her. Finally Susan makes it out. Paul. He's been arrested. Jan thrusts her tablet into Susan's hands, presses play. Look at that, she says triumphantly. Sure enough, there Paul is, walking onto the ramp of the police barge, handcuffed, flanked by two men in suits. Susan feels conflicted. *He's still denying it,* says Jan with derision. *Says it's all circumstantial, a coincidence.* The two women look at each other. Not very likely.

The two women talk for upwards of an hour, while Rob heads out to the backyard to pull the lantana that keeps coming back despite their best efforts. When Jan excuses herself to go to the toilet, Susan's eyes fall upon her scrapbook, sitting on the kitchen table. She sees Rob outside. Susan has a sudden impulse. She turns to the back page,

Television, works well, $300 ono, call Rob. She dials the number, presses the phone close to her ear, listens intently as it begins to ring. Looking out the window, she watches as Rob reaches into his back pocket, answers his phone.

Susan is astonished. She drops the handset with a clatter as all the rage she has held onto these past few weeks rushes to the surface. The screen door slams behind her, and she stalks out to near the back shed where Rob is surveying the yard. The walk from her house to the back fence takes an instant. *You listed my television for sale,* Susan says, furious. Her voice is shaking, but she's sure about what she's saying, surer than she's ever been. Rob looks alarmed at this sudden confrontation, takes a step back. *What are you talking about?* he says, confused. *Don't lie,* she snaps back, *I saw you answer your phone.* A flash of recognition crosses Rob's face, but he quickly covers it up. *You're not making any sense,* he says.

For the first time since this all began, Susan doesn't doubt herself or wonder if she has read the situation correctly. The power she has given away has returned. *Give me my money back,* she says, slowly, enunciating every word. She lays it out to Rob. *You lied about the price of the television you bought, and now you're lying about selling my old one.*

Rob is impassive, unreadable. A sense of unease comes over Susan. She was expecting an instant retort. After a pause, he says, *I'd be careful about accusing people of things with no proof,* his voice steady and firm. Susan wavers for a moment. Before she can answer, the screen door bangs, and the two of them turn to see Jan motioning for them to come back inside. She's too far away to hear what they're saying but Susan sees a flicker of fear cross Rob's face. *Don't tell Jan,* he orders her in a low voice.

Susan hesitates and fumbles for the right words but regains her footing, her strength. *Give me my money back and I won't have to,* she hears herself saying. Susan loathes Rob for forcing her into this role. All

Susan wants is to be repaid, for Rob to stop doing whatever this is. There must be a word for what is happening between them, but it eludes her.

Rob makes a split second decision. *Fine,* he says. Jan, impatient now, calls out to them. *Susan, come inside! We've got more to talk about.* It's the same moment that Rob finishes his reply to Susan and says under his breath, *fuckin' bitch.*

Susan looks at him in shock. Thoughts of Paul being led off the island in handcuffs flash through her mind. Rob is a good twenty years older than Paul, but Susan notices for the first time how similar the two men look, the likeness between them. She understands now how it could escalate. She gazes at him, at first with curiosity that morphs into hostility, staring him down. He seems uncomfortable, looks away.

Without taking her eyes off of Rob, Susan calls back to Jan, *I'm coming.*

KEREN HEENAN is the winner of a number of Australian short story awards and a winner of the Griffith Review Novella Project 2019. She has been published in Australian journals and anthologies, and in anthologies and online in the US, UK and Ireland.

Murmuration

KEREN HEENAN

On his way back from the garden, Vinnie sees she's there again at the window, one hand holding the curtain aside. He thinks she's probably seen him seeing her; her head jolts back then the curtain closes with a jerk. Vinnie senses she's still there though, behind the fabric, huddled near the wall. There's a thin line of light between the curtains, some movement, a shadow.

Vinnie had only moved in a few months ago. He'd knocked on doors looking for like-minded folk who could steer him in the direction of community allotments, reclaimed idle spaces where gardens could thrive. There was one already established, within walking distance. Saved him filling in forms, applying for grants or sponsorship. The woman at the window was the only one who hadn't answered his knock but he knew she was there. Could see her shadow behind the dimpled glass panel. Any number of reasons occurred to him for not answering a knock from a stranger, so he didn't think too much about it. Until he realised later that he'd rarely seen her apart from through her window, or peering through the slender gap between the door jamb and door as if she may take the plunge and come out.

The front of her place is a study in half-realised potential: a line of bricks in a sweeping arc that stops abruptly, weeds threading their way between the bricks, grass long and unkempt either side. It's as if there had once been a plan, a grand design of some sort for a garden bed, or a path, now forgotten. The house is a pale yellow, colour faded and paint peeling off. One corner of the front wall has been painted a slate grey, fresh and clean. Another plan perhaps, going nowhere now. He wonders about this as he passes. Opens the gate to his own little rented weatherboard next door.

When he'd first moved there, he thought the house next door must have been empty. Then once, on a sleepless night when he'd gone out to the front verandah for a cigarette, something he did rarely now, he'd seen her checking her mail well after midnight. He'd pulled back behind the yuccas so as not to alarm her but he saw her head lift, turn, lift again, as if she'd smelt the smoke, then she hurried inside. He'd thought of his mother, after his father had gone: sitting staring into silence, not dressing for the day, lying around in her grubby pink dressing-gown with daytime television blaring but no one watching. She'd pulled herself together eventually, with help from family, friends. This woman though, she was more like someone who didn't know the pandemic had passed, at least for long enough to allow some movement, some progress and clawing back of what had once been. She was like a soldier holed up on an island not knowing the war was over, that there was no need to scurry away from an approaching boat.

Vinnie's house is small. But he's used to small. There's plenty of space in the sunroom down the back for his workshop and storage. He dumps the bags on the bench and puts the kettle on. Looks out at the shuttered window of the woman's house, the peeling paint, broken down-pipe.

He'd asked Joe, from down the street, about her but his only response was, "She's a bit weird. Never see her. The people who lived in your house sometimes gave her food and stuff. After her hubby died. He was okay, nice bloke." And Vinnie thought of his mother again — all his creeping around her, as if her stillness would just go away if he left it unacknowledged. He wonders how his mother would've coped back then had she been faced with a pandemic and enforced isolation.

Quarantine had changed the way Vinnie thought about life, about work, animals, about people and how things work out when everyone pulls together. He'd been out on the hill behind his old place, looking at the city in the distance, wondering how everyone was coping there with the second wave of lockdown. Wondering whether he was ready to move back there when things had calmed down a bit. The open space and vastness of the sky, the veggie garden he'd created from a yellowed and dry patch of earth, the metal sculptures he'd made and positioned around the place, piles of found and recycled items — junk to most people, art materials to Vinnie. All this he could give up for a place where there were people, bouncing ideas around, creating links between each other. For Vinnie, quarantine had been alienating and disturbingly still. Not the godsend it had been for some who revelled in being left alone in their own space. Vinnie found he had no new ideas, no buzz of satisfaction. What was the point, when tomorrow was always sliding around, shapeless and slippery. Neither his art nor his garden gave him solace anymore.

On the hill out there that evening, with the wind tossing his hair about, the sun dipping low to the hills, he'd seen the birds. Dance-like in their syncopation, flowing as one, the sum of its parts all working together. He watched them wheel and swoop, darkening the sky as they turned then almost disappearing as their wings dipped further. Individuals working hard to achieve an overall shape. One little movement, he'd thought, then they're all moving together like it's been choreographed. He stared up at their swooping harmony while the salmon sky turned to mauve. He wasn't achieving anything living out in the hills like a hermit. He may as well be living on some island in the middle of the deep, wild blue. Just him, the wind, the churning sea. When it was possible to do so, he'd move back to the city. People, colour and movement would give him a new start. Community, he liked that word, liked the shape of it.

Vinnie takes his coffee and the plastic bags out to the workshop. Starts to sort the contents into appropriate tubs: metals, plastics, lids, miscellaneous, rubbish. If he can avoid it he never buys materials for his projects, it's all recycled or found objects. Mav, from the garden, had been saving plastic lids, gave Vinnie a whole bag full because he didn't know what to do with them. Vinnie's working on a large-scale mandala on reclaimed timber with metal lids and bright coloured plastics cut to shape. He plans on working with a primary school in the area to create one for their garden project. They've given him a couple of weeks to come up with a submission. It's a paid gig, he thinks that might open doors for him. He wants to make sure it looks okay first, that he knows what the pitfalls are and what the kids would be capable of doing. They're only little kids, he doubts whether they could wield a hammer without stuffing something up, or worse, smashing their tiny fingers. They can glue things on, he'll hammer them later and they'll think it's all their own work anyway.

Vinnie's seen into the woman's back yard, over the fence. Piles of wood, iron scraps, old car parts. He'd love to get in there and have a good rummage around. Won't do it without asking her first. But they're not on those sorts of neighbourly terms. He thinks of the flock of birds moving into those shapes together, no telepathic connection, no magic between the birds. All it takes is for each bird to check the small group of birds around it and respond within a couple of wing flaps to neighbours' movements. Vinnie would like to be able to bring the woman next door back into the *flock*. Everyone should be part of a whole. But knocking on her door and asking if he can rummage around in her junk is probably not the way to go.

He remembers how strange it was at first — knocking on doors, approaching the school, fumbling his way through, *hello, I've just moved in, wondering if . . .* After all that time on his own, speaking to the birds, the air, himself, it had been like he'd lost the art of communication. He'd had to force himself, not listen to the echo of his words, just keep going, keep knocking and talking, and eventually the edges of his words became rounded, smoother, more his and less some other fumbling stranger's. He wonders if it would be like this for the woman next door as well.

Later that night the rain hits, sudden and squally, pounding the roof like giant needles flung from the sky. Vinnie lets the noise surround him, waits for the roll of thunder after a flash of lightning. Then over the steady tattoo of rain, the *whoomph* of wind under the eaves, there's a faint wailing like a baby crying or perhaps a small dog howling. He lies still a moment, and there it is again — a low wailing, a pause, then it starts up again. He kicks off the blankets, pulls on trousers and a jumper and takes his coat from the back door.

Outside in the yard he hears it louder now, coming from next door. He steps up onto the railing and looks over the fence. Lightning cleaves the sky and in the sudden glare he sees her. Sitting on the ground, face white and round, her eyes closed. In a single movement he bounds over the fence without thinking how this would appear to her.

She staggers to her feet, mouth a wailing "O", tries to run and slips. He reaches her and puts out his hands to help her up. She rocks from side to side, hands to her ears, and he pushes his hands under her arms, hoists her up. She's small and thin and he lifts her easily. Puts his arm under her knees and carries her like wet sheets to the back door.

Inside he puts her down, steadies her. There's a light from the hallway, but no light in the room and he fumbles at the wall for a switch. She staggers as if drunk, flinching from the burst of light as he locates the switch, and she stumbles backwards. "I'm sorry," he says. "I didn't mean to frighten you, but I heard you … thought you might be hurt. Are you?" He watches her mouth move but no words form. He can't tell how old she might be, maybe fifty, sixty, he's no good at guessing ages. Her eyes are piercingly blue, and she plucks at the sodden dressing-gown wrapped around her.

She reaches out, her fingers splayed as if to stop him, push him away. She limps towards the chair and sits. "Please go away," she says finally, "I'm okay." But she doesn't look okay and Vinnie takes a half step towards her, thinks better of it and stops. She puts her hand out again. "Just go," she whispers, then louder, "I rolled my ankle. It hurt. I was annoyed, but I'm okay."

"Do you want ice, I can …" he looks at the fridge.

"No!" She shakes her head, her wet, greying hair is plastered to her skull and loose droplets sprinkle from the ends.

What the hell was she doing outside in that weather anyway, Vinnie wonders. As if she's read his mind, she says, "I was getting something from the line, I slipped …" and she waves her hand before resting it on her ankle. "Please," she says, and dismisses him with another wave of her hand.

"Sure," Vinnie says, backing towards the door. "I'm next door, if you need anything, with your ankle, you know, like that. Vinnie, the name's Vinnie." She doesn't offer her name, and he leaves, the door banging closed behind him.

The next morning when he wakes, he wonders whether her meltdown in the yard in the rain had been a sort of cry for help. Had he left her alone too easily? He imagines her there in her kitchen, staring at the door after he'd left, waiting for him to return perhaps, tell her how she can do it — get herself out of the pit she's in. Then again, he'd often jumped into things without thinking. What the hell must have gone through her mind when she looked up and saw him there in the storm and the dark like that.

He puts his lunch — a muesli bar and fruit and bread — into his backpack, crams in plastic bags for rubbish pick-up and leaves for the garden. Passing the woman's house, he glances at the long and scraggly grass in the yard. Imagines snakes lurking there in summer, frowns, tucks the thought away.

The garden is only a ten-minute walk, a triangle of green between the railway line and the road. The streets are quiet, just a couple of rainbow lorikeets squawking from a flowering gum over a fence. It's usually quiet here in the back streets, though there's a constant hum of traffic from the main highway away to the left. Not quite the buzz it probably used to be, in pre-Covid days, but it's winding back up again. Not as many cafes apparently, some struggled during the lockdown and never returned.

Mav and Jess are there already, picking the broad beans. Mav holds one out for him. "Here, sweet as," he says. "Don't forget to take some home with you, everyone else has got theirs. D'ya want to thin out the carrot seedlings, then we can get the trench ready for the asparagus, yeah?"

"Sure," Vinnie says.

Jess calls out, "You finished that scarecrow thingie yet?"

"No, not yet. I will but. Soon." He pictures the metal creature he'd started soldering together, unsure of its final shape until he'd gone a little further, sorted through his metals pile. Then he'd become focused on trying to get the mandala finished, excited by the possibility of working on the school project. He'll get back to it though. The birds had destroyed the pomegranates this year and they'd do the same with the fig tree when it fruits. He's glad Jess has asked about it. She can be a bit cool towards him, a bit prickly, not quite as welcoming as Mav and the others. He'd heard on the garden-grapevine that Jess hadn't really wanted a stranger to join the collective. She'd been outvoted though. He doesn't want to come across as someone who promises things and never delivers. He'll get onto it. Tonight.

He finishes with the carrot seedlings and puts some liquid fertiliser on the leeks. Helps Jess and Mav with the asparagus trench, filling it with compost and manure. They have a break. The three of them sit and eat, chatting about what they're going to do about the rats, or is it possums — they're never sure but something's doing a job on the peas and the cabbages. A train passes and they watch until it rocks around the bend and slows into the station. After the rain last night, everywhere is wet and shining in the sun. Vinnie thinks he could just sit there with his eyes closed and doze for hours. But he wants to get back, there's a couple of things he needs to do.

Back home, he borrows Joe's lawnmower. Writes a note and slips it under the woman's door — *I'm going to mow your grass, I hope that's okay, I'm worried about snakes with summer warming up now. Vinnie, from next door.*

As soon as the mower kicks into action he imagines her in there, head up, alert — *who's that, what's that!* He expects her at the door or window any moment, keeps glancing over to check. But she doesn't appear and he finishes the job. Returns Joe's mower, then settles in front of the metal creature in his workshop, looking at it from all sides. Nods, "You're a bit of a dragon, I think," he mutters, picturing the flames as cloth or plastics moving in the wind. He spends the remainder of the day working on it, thinking he'll have to get Mav to bring his ute to pick it up, it'll be too heavy to carry.

He takes a handful of broad beans from the fridge, puts them in a bag and leaves them on the woman's front step. When he checks, the bag is still there that evening. Too much, he thinks. She mightn't even like beans.

Mav picks him up the next day and they hoist the dragon into the back of the ute and take it to the garden. Jess and some of the others are there when they arrive. Jess raises her eyebrows and gives a little nod when she sees it. "Not your average scarecrow," she says. Vinnie takes it as an understated compliment. Together they position the dragon near the pomegranate tree and tie the strips of cloth and plastic to the hooks inside its jaws. On cue, a breeze blows up and the strips of red and yellow rustle and ripple out like a kite's tail.

On his way home he notices the bag of beans is gone from the woman's step.

The next morning, in his mailbox, a note: *Thank you*, in neat cursive script. He gives a tiny wave with his fingers towards the house as if she's there at the door. One little movement, he's thinking. One little wing flap.

REG LYNCH has worked for nearly forty years as an editorial illustrator and cartoonist for newspapers and magazines — he must have created thousands of them in that time. Each one is a single frame micro story with a setting, characters, tone, timing and mostly (but not always) dialogue and usually with a smile attached. Very occasionally, he would be asked to write a small piece for some publication or other and enjoyed moving outside his allocated frame.

Since moving from Sydney to North West Tasmania ten years ago he found he was writing a lot more and enjoying it a lot. He collected so much stuff in his head over time, time to use it. When his wife, Nerissa, mentioned this competition to him and that the theme was "Island", he immediately pictured the final line, then worked back from there.

Reg currently contributes an opinion cartoon every Sunday in the Sydney Morning Herald.

A man's home
is his jumping castle

REG LYNCH

Currawong is a little old town huddled along both sides of a minor river in regional Australia. Travelling away from it along Old Currawong Road, the passing landscape's only breathtaking feature is the sheer enormity of its lack of breathtaking features. Needless to say, like a lot of this country, it is flat.

Big sky, scrubby trees, sheds in the half distance, scattered paddocks penning scattered sheep. Occasional shaded homes at the end of long gravel driveways. Flat, and hot looking.

But wait.

About eight kilometres out, on the right, off beyond that mid distance, is a hill. It is like a child's drawing of a hill. After the preceding enormous lack, its eccentricity generates a smile. Half a coconut on a khaki tablecloth.

A little further along the main road, directly in line with the hill, at the head of one of those long straight driveways, stands a letter box made from an ancient meat safe. Welded on top, roughly cut from plate metal, is the silhouette of a bending palm tree. Both were once shiny white. A faded number and name painted on the side: 231 McKay.

At the other end of this gravel drive is a rambling big flat house surrounded by vehicles and machinery and tin sheds and weeds and an air of surrender.

A phone is ringing in the house. It rings for quite a while before silencing itself, unanswered.

The house is cool and dark inside and, compared with outside, it is surprisingly neat and orderly, comfortable and pleasant.

Bill McKay is standing inside his back screen door looking out through the limp mesh. This yard out here and round the side has more stuff scattered about. Dead water tanks, a few more cars, a few more sheds, an abandoned excavator. An overgrown outdoor setting cowers by the collapsing back fence under the big gum tree.

But he is looking past all this to that hill across the paddocks. The phone begins to ring again and he picks up his hat, pushes open the door and steps out into the heat. Bill walks the cracked cement path down to the back gate and sets off across those paddocks.

Bill is a trim sort of guy. In his seventies but you wouldn't know. The only clue maybe is his sagging bottom eyelids revealing that vulnerable looking red shiny crescent that old folks get, making them appear bewildered. He sports a white moustache that was black forty years ago when he grew it for a bet with his father Eric.

He was nearly thirty then, and when the mo was grown, his father suddenly died. Here in one of the sheds. The day that the fumes got him. *The Day the Earth Stood Still*, Bill calls it to himself.

Up until that day Bill had been planning to leave here. Ever since the very first time he climbed up the hill by himself aged seven and looked out far away beyond the flatness to vague, alluring mirages of the distant places he'd go to, Bill had been planning to leave here. That particular day though, before his poor mother found his father dead, Bill was *really* ready to go. An opportunity had lined up for him, a future. The Islands. Tickets booked even. Not to be. Mirage.

He had spent a sizeable part of his early life on top of that hill. Looking out, imagining, planning. Stubby grass sprinkled with granite boulders, a few wind-bent trees here and there. Animal burrows, droppings. It was comically symmetrical, a rising rounded hemisphere. Its circumference would have fitted snugly onto the field at a first-class cricket stadium. The summit would be up level with the roof on the top deck of the stands.

Before the day the earth stood still, he used to go up there four or five times a week. Now he hardly goes up at all because each time he does, his heart breaks. These days he only stares at it through the back door wire.

Bill bore no grudge against his father for dying. Similarly he never felt trapped into staying with, then caring for, his widowed mum until she too finally died. He didn't have to stay. His lively mum Nancy had seemed to cope well with the sudden tragedy at first, sudden tragedies being quite common amongst country folk, but after a few years she just petered out. Drifted away from her friends and neighbours and her office job at Currawong council and cloistered herself in front of the television, reinventing herself as a hypochondriac.

Julia, his older sister who'd left home and married shortly before Eric's death, had told Bill for years and years to put their mum into a nice place and just go. They could afford it.

The McKays were pretty well off, you see. In Currawong in the '70s, Eric had opened an automotive repair business. Cars and tractors. He was one of those people who could fix anything, solve any puzzle. Then a petrol station, then a tyre service. He watched them grow, kept up with the times. He was making a lot of money but always kept that old-school mechanic's pride in quality work. Honest, canny and successful.

Bill had worked happily alongside his dad from when he was old enough to pick up a car battery, so after Eric's death it seemed natural to carry on, keeping the businesses going and growing. Honestly, cannily, successfully. He didn't have his father's magical knack with machinery but he knew his way around a workshop, was good with figures, employed good staff and treated them well. Everybody happy.

He had no friends though, and still doesn't. The only time he ever really felt comfortable with anyone was with himself, up there.

He approaches the foot of the hill, reaches it and stops. Stands, hands on hips. From his shirt pocket he removes a little spiral notepad and pen. He doesn't attempt to climb the hill today. Instead, he turns to his left and begins to pace alongside its perimeter, measuring.

. . .

"He's bought a jumping castle."

"A what?"

The two blokes were sitting by a window in the front bar of the Woolpack Hotel in town. The tall one dressed in grubby hi-vis overalls, the other in a worn blue checked flannelette shirt and jeans. Identical boots and beers.

Hi-vis explained, "You know, those big blow-up things the kids jump up and down on. Shaped like a castle."

"Oh right. Really?"

"And the pump. Harry was telling me. Bill come to Harry's farm sale last Saturday. Got real excited when he saw it, took it away."

"Huh. Always been a bit different old Bill."

"I drove by his place Wednesday morning and saw him out in the weeds tinkering with the guts of that ancient digger. He was still on the tools when I come back after lunch."

"That piece of crap. That's not run in years."

"I know."

"Huh. Did he buy anything else weird off Harry?"

"Nah. I reckon there'd already be at least one of everything he'd ever need stashed in those sheds of his."

"I reckon. Except a jumping castle obviously."

"Obviously," says hi-vis as he stands up from the table and points at the empty glasses. "Beer, I imagine?"

. . .

There was indeed at least one of everything Bill needed in those sheds. The jumping castle was what you'd call an impulse buy. It spoke to him. The cherry on top as it were.

A sheet of butchers paper was thumbtacked to a cork board hanging adjacent to a work bench in the second-newest of the sheds. Bill sat, resting his bent elbow on the bench, his fist supporting his head, his face supporting a grin as he gazed at his plan.

A simple diagram. A bird's eye view. In the top right corner, a curly depiction of the kink in the river which touches the eastern border of his property. A dotted line leads from there to meet the circumference of a large circle drawn perfunctorily onto the left half of the page. The dotted line is labeled "827 metres". The circle's circumference reads "487 metres". "(3 wide)" it says as well. Next to that, underlined, is written *5-6 Days.*

At the bottom of the paper is a lengthy list written in a column. Most items have been crossed off. Tonight he was moving the resurrected excavator down to the dark side of the hill to sit with the other gear. Last night he'd laid out the 827 metres of flexible irrigation pipe up from the riverbank.

7-8 days later, Bill McKay is standing inside his back screen door looking out through the limp mesh to – then the phone rings. He glances up at the kitchen clock. Midday on the dot. He moves across, drops his notepad onto the breakfast bench and sits on a stool. He reaches for the handset.

"Mr Smith, I presume."

Smiles.

"Yes, I admire punctuality. How's the hunt?"

Bill doodles on his pad as he listens.

"That's fantastic news! I knew you'd be the man for the job. How many?"

A broad grin spreads across his face.

"Six! Fantastic. And size-wise?"

He nods and smiles and looks out across the paddocks through the window above the sink.

"Yes, everything's ready this end. When should I expect you?"

He writes down *MON pm.*

"Monday night? Perfect. You know where to come? Where my place is?"

He nods to the phone

"Oh that's right, yes. Was that really twenty years ago?"

He turns over to a fresh page on the pad, pen poised, eyebrows raised.

"Yes it certainly does, doesn't it? Yes. Well now Mr Smith, about payment. All up, how much do I owe you, and what are your bank details so I can …"

His eyebrows settle down as Mr Smith answers.

"Oh, of course, of course. In your line of work, I understand."

Bill nods and shakes his head alternately.

"No, it's not exactly, is it?"

Smiles and listens. On the small page he writes a not insubstantial figure preceded by a dollar sign.

"No problems, I'll have it here for you."

Smiles and listens again.

"OK Mr Smith, thanks for calling and I'll see you Monday night, it's usually pretty well dark by about eight."

Bill stands up.

"Yep. See you then. Good. Thanks again."

Bill hangs up and exhales big-time. He happily rubs his palms together as he walks into the lounge room. The television is on.

As usual, Bill'd had his coffee and biscuits watching an episode of whatever vintage program was currently being repeated in the mornings. It was *I Dream Of Jeannie* at present. He hadn't meant to leave it on. He didn't like leaving it on.

It was showing the midday news that he didn't want to hear or see. He turned his back on it, grabbed up the remote, shut the power off and walked out.

There was a stack of taped-up cardboard cartons in the front room. A couple of small side tables. A lamp. It wasn't a big stack, just family stuff mainly. A few precious things, heirlooms. One or two examples of dad's classic tools. Some interesting clothes and books. Photographs. Things that sister Julia and her kids and their families might want to go through one day. Some blokes with a truck are coming this afternoon to take it away to a storage place in the big city. The rest of the stuff in the house?

Bill turns away and returns to the kitchen to retrieve and pocket his notepad. Rubbing his palms together again he whistles a jaunty tune as he pushes through the screen door and heads into the second newest shed where he rests himself against the bench and stares contentedly at his pinned up plan.

The circle now has a small wonky castle drawn in its centre, and the underlined *5-6 Days* had been scribbled out. The dotted line from the river has been coloured in blue, as has the circumference of the circle. He picks up and uncaps a black felt-tip pen and leans in close to the bottom of the paper.

"Thank yooouuuu, Mr Smith", he croons quietly to himself as he draws a line through the last item on the checklist.

"Bull sharks."

STEPHEN MAY is an awarded copywriter in the world of advertising (yes, the dark arts). He lives in Sydney and has been copywriting for over 16 years. Recently, he has begun to write short stories and is enjoying creating work longer than 30 seconds. During the pandemic he found himself reading a lot more. One day he'd like to pen a novel and be classed as a "real writer" following in the footsteps of Jane Caro, Peter Carey, Bryce Courtenay, and Robert Hughes — who all used to be copywriters in the ad game.

Island life

STEPHEN MAY

Eventually our worlds shrink, and we end up on our own little islands. Over time, the edges of our continents erode, forcing us backwards until we can touch the shoreline in every direction without even moving. What once were puddles between us and others grow into oceans, and so there's no more skipping to the people we love.

As the distance continues to expand, our strength to take on the currents and swim to neighbouring lands diminishes even further. Over time water becomes custard then wet cement, fatiguing us to a point where we give up even trying.

So, we age and deteriorate, left with no choice but to exist on an ever-shrinking island, stranded, staring bitterly at a horizon that has discourteously wedged itself between now and the life we once ruled. Its advance is relentless.

She is a wife, mother, grandmother, great grandmother — and she is my aunty. Her island is in an aged-care archipelago on the south coast of New South Wales housing a fluctuating number of around sixty residents. A neat complex, it is single-storey with metal and wooden railings pinstriping the walls. Carpets are patterned to disguise spills. Couches are patterned to disguise style. The walls are beige, and the skirting boards and cornices are finished in calming salmon.

Her room is through a gaping doorway in the "The Ocean View Wing". There is no ocean view from her room, but you can see a slither of water from the library. Her room is a shade darker than the common areas, nudging the colour of the caramel topping they pump onto her ice cream from bulky plastic dispensers (in here, the flamboyance of famous condiment labels is gone, replaced by tall commercial bar codes).

Next to the sliding door to her balcony sits a small selection of familiar trinkets and photos, huddled and frightened on their foreign shelf. Other homely touches such as doilies and patchwork blankets do their best to make the space feel familiar but are not effective enough to hide the fact that this is a medical facility.

She is there because cancer took her left leg just below the knee and is now knocking on the door of her right leg. For 97 years she moved as she wanted. A fierce independence had taken her around the world. She raised a family and was now the very last of her generation on the tree.

Only two years earlier the cancer was spotted infiltrating her body, and her world began to shrink. Cruelly, it attacked her foot, making it difficult to move, robbing her of the ability to walk up and down stairs. Unable to make the climb to the second storey of the home she shared with her daughter and son-in-law, she was stranded on the ground floor, unless she was carried. The tide of final life had begun lapping her shoreline.

Before long, even the short walk from the kitchen to the bedroom was problematic and painful with her left calf bear-trapped by gangrene, leaving her to exist within a couple of measly rooms. Her continent was no more.

In January, the lower part of her leg was removed, and with it her independence. It marooned her on a rectangular island of cold steel and foam in a nursing home where the floor may as well not exist. The ground is now just a spatial element to be observed, as untouchable as the stars. Her bed is Alcatraz. All she can do is look out, which, for her, is essentially staring into a thick fog thanks to severely deteriorated eyesight. They should change the word from cancer to prisoner. It steals freedom. It steals everything.

Audio books help her pass the time, at least spiritually transporting her off her padded isle. But they too become monotonous.

Unfortunately, with her faculties very much unimpaired, her days are spent in a constant state of frustration, waiting to sleep and forget time. Morphine helps. It kills physical pain and can also quash the boredom once her eyes are closed. It knocks her out, allowing her to live fruitfully in her dreams. Life is flipped. Dreaming is one way to leave the island, death is the other.

Only those around her with dementia seem to be oblivious to life on their tiny pockets of land. Awake, but in a sense sleeping, they spend their days doddering on the shoreline, unaware of the rising waters, playing in the wet sands just as they did as children. Do the feeble-minded live a better existence when this close to mortality? Unfortunately, no one's ever lost their marbles then found them again to tell us if this is true.

Islands like hers are difficult to visit. Even more so during a pandemic. The isolation of lockdown was another blow. Having family amputated was just as agonising as losing a limb. For months and months, the only way to communicate with loved ones in nursing homes was by phone, which came with its own challenges when calling my aunty because of dodgy hearing and vocal cords. That shoreline, it keeps being whittled away.

She jokes of dying. Of wanting to go. Being done with it all. That she arrived too early at heaven's gate only to be told to sit in a room and wait until she's called. Her mind is still nimble enough to commentate the pain of her situation using dry humour.

With visitation restrictions still heavily enforced, only a select few can visit. Then, once inside, you learn that for most of her neighbours there is no select few, restrictions or not. That for a million reasons, not a single soul will visit them until the day of their funeral.

Freedom is often depicted as standing at the top of a famous mountain or sailing seas. Or a trite walk along the beach or tickling the heads of wheat as you run through an open field at sunset. Or a car on a highway powering along Route 66. Swimming with dolphins. Skydiving.

But to truly understand what freedom is, away from the cliches, you must fly to someone you love who has none.

You become a bird.

Just as a magpie flies into prison grounds and leaves as it wishes, so too do we when we visit compounds for the aged. To her, and others living in these places, we aren't merely walking in, we are flying — just as she once had the ability to do before her wings were clipped. As nonchalantly as the lorikeets that land and take-off from her balcony railing each afternoon, we periodically migrate to these islands, perch, then take flight once again.

And so I make the flight to her island. Once perched we reminisce, and I wonder if it's actually the right thing to be doing. Her every day is thinking about the years behind her. Gone are goals and dreams of future. Who cares what's around the corner when your body won't allow you to peek around it? All you have is what you've done, not what you're yet do. So, tinged in melancholy, we converse about good times and last night's dinner, because there's no use talking about a tomorrow she doesn't want. Conversation is a Catch 22. But at least the act talking makes her feel better and kills some time.

She is from the generation of politeness. While the staff are familiar to her now, there is always formality with how she converses with them, not wanting to rock the boat or put them out in any way. In her failing eyes, she is an inconvenience. Using a hoist, they crane her to the bath and place her on the toilet. It's mechanical and humiliating for a woman so ladylike. Then she remembers she was once a nurse herself, so begrudgingly she surrenders to their helping hands.

And still she remains stoic, resigned to the reality that soon her other leg will need to be removed. I wonder if she cries when I am not there. She'd never cry in front of me or anyone. She is from the stiff upper lip generation, the bite your tongue, grin and bear it, suck it up generation. Yes, I'm sure she cries when I am not there.

Two hours pass quickly. I've learnt the routine of mealtime – which are sandwich days, and which are roast beef days. I make her laugh as best I can. I've caught up on which of her neighbours have passed on. She lists them like a teacher calling the roll at school, emotionless with a tinge of sorrow. What's the point of becoming close to people who are destined to break your heart so quickly?

Before I fly from her island, I faintly kiss her forehead. Her skin is so fragile now that even reckless pressure from lips can bruise. Hugging could cause serious injury. This is how cancer hurts everyone.

I take off, leaving her behind. Part of me is glad to get the hell out of there. I glide past the rooms of people even closer to death and consider how lucky I am to still have my wings. In the back of my mind, I know that one day I'll exist on an island like theirs, too (I fly away faster).

Until then, all we can do is sandbag our shores the best we can. Keep the sovereignty of our continents robust and heavily fortified. Because no matter how invincible we consider our empires to be, little by little they all eventually decay under the weight of age. While we have the wings to fly, we must soar to those who have none.

I called her this evening.

As usual, it was difficult to hear through the scratchy late 90s handset she was holding as gravity caused it to slowly worm through her fingers, pushing the speaker onto her neck. A soft voice on a scratchy and muffled phone. After a while, you learn to pick up the gist of conversation with every third or fourth word. And if you're still not sure, you give an affirmative answer until you're able to decipher.

Sadly, another neighbour passed away overnight. It was a man with dementia who would walk into the women's rooms mistaking the female residents for his beloved wife. He'd take their hand, sit with them, sing to them, and often try climbing into bed with them. Those with clear minds, like my aunt, humour him and call for staff assistance.

On the shrivelled grapevine she heard that the gentleman across the hallway, who would often yell obscenities then apologise, was probably next to go. She joked about running a betting book on it all and cleaning up. If anyone could, it would be her.

Sunday lunch was roast beef, gravy and roast vegetables. For this they wheelchaired her into the main dining room where she sat and enjoyed her meal with a couple of familiar faces. The potatoes were especially delicious, which is code for 'nice and soft so they're easy to chew with dentures'. Dessert the following night was ice cream with topping, the highlight being whipped cream (in a nursing home whipped cream is what cocaine is to an addict). It was the talk of the town. Tuesday night there was a cricket match on the television, so she switched it on and listened, looking towards the soft green haze of the screen. She began a new audio book, too — a crime story with plenty of murdering.

One of the residents visited her room offering to cut her fringe, assuring my aunty she was a skilled hairdresser. As it turns out, she was never a skilled hairdresser. Like a child playing pretend, she had a pair of scissors and decided hair artistry was her calling and cruised the corridors prospecting new customers. The staff weren't happy knowing she'd been carrying scissors. Luckily, it was relatively simple for them to retrace the rogue stylist's steps following a trail of bad hair cuts. They have booked in my aunty, along with others, to have warped fringes straightened and patches blended by the resident hairdresser.

The doctor visited. The news is not good but was expected. The right leg is beginning to show signs of gangrene and is sorer, in spite of the morphine. Though her eyes are faulty, she can still make out the inky blue blotches that are moving across her swollen ankle. She knows it won't be long before it too will need amputation.

Her island shrinks a little more.

TERRY MULHERN is a writer who splits his time between Somerset, in northwest Tasmania, and Melbourne. Terry's writing spans themes of Tasmanian history, ecology, and culture.

Terry was a joint winner of the 2020-21 Van Diemen History Prize for his essay "Insubordination and Improper Intimacy". His 2018-19 entry, "St Valentine's Tears" was highly commended. He has also published in FortySouth Tasmania, Science Write Now, Pursuit *and the* Papers and Proceedings of the Royal Society of Tasmania.

Born in north Queensland, Terry has worked at universities in the UK and around Australia, but his heart is in north-west Tasmania.

The satchel

TERRY MULHERN

PORTSMOUTH HARBOUR, JUNE 1801

Henry dipped the oars into the water and began to row. The shore receded from him and the little boat picked up speed, slipping out into the deeper water away from the sedges and reeds ringing the shore. Today, Henry's strokes seemed fuller and stronger. It was his eleventh birthday. At last, begrudgingly, his father had given him permission to venture alone much further out into the broad estuary. But he was not to go near the hulks.

"I'll not have you gift some damned Frenchie prisoner my boat and have him row it away across the Channel!"

As Henry approached Pewit Island, he disturbed the swarms of waders and seabirds strutting and bobbing about on the mudflats.

Plovers, godwits, terns, and black-headed gulls wheeled overhead, their shrill cries ringing in his ears. The boat scraped bottom and he jumped out, sinking deeply into the soft mud. He grabbed the rope coiled in the bow and dragged the boat up as close to the shore as he could. When the boat would move no further, he pulled his leather satchel over his shoulder and trudged the last twenty yards to the island. Henry made the rope fast to the twisted trunk of a stunted shrub, just beyond the piles of shingle at the high tide mark.

He walked to the highest point of the island and found a place to sit. Henry unbuckled his satchel and pulled out the bread and cheese wrapped in a cloth that cook had given him for his dinner. He ate half, saving the rest for later. Then he sat admiring the satchel. His mother had given it to him that morning. Over and over, he ran his fingertips across the carvings on the front flap, then traced the letters of the monogram – "H.H."

Some weeks earlier, while wandering through the stalls of Portchester market, Betsy Hellyer paused to peruse the wares manufactured by the French prisoners. Inlaid wooden boxes, carved bone domino sets, intricately woven straw baskets and leather work. She was about to move on when she spied the satchel. Betsy knew at once this was what she wanted for her Henry. How many times had her dreamy boy set off in sunshine to draw in the woods or by the seashore, only to return home in the rain, his beloved drawings soggy and ruined?

Betsy knew she shouldn't have favourites, but she saw so much of herself in Henry. His love of nature and books and his thirst for knowledge. She loved all thirteen of her children, but Henry's gentleness touched her soul in a way none of the others did. Anyway, John favoured the eldest, William, to such an extent that anything Betsy did for Henry paled into insignificance.

She picked up the satchel and examined it closely. It was cleverly designed and neatly made. Robust and functional, as well as beautiful.

The front flap was handsomely decorated with carved oak leaves and meadow flowers encircling the space for a monogram. The French prisoner of war, seated nearby, acknowledged her interest in the satchel.

"Le cartable, aimes-tu, Madame?"

"Oui, Monsieur," replied Betsy, who then, in effortless French, complimented him on his fine workmanship. The Frenchman was pleased that a Lady, clearly both well-educated and wealthy, was attracted by his wares. He explained how such a weatherproof satchel was essential to protect an officer's papers and maps, and how his satchels and saddlebags were highly valued in his regiment.

Preliminaries done, they haggled over the price. He started outrageously high, and she embarrassingly low. After an enjoyable bout, with much parrying and ripostes, they settled to their mutual satisfaction. The artisan gestured at the space for the monogram.

"Quelles initiales, Madame?"

Henry extracted his pencils and sketchbook from one of the oilcloth-lined compartments of the satchel. From his vantage point, he scanned the horizon for the view that most took his fancy. First, the chalk ridgeline of Portsdown Hill caught his eye. But he dismissed it and turned to the south. In the distance was the forest of masts of the naval squadron. Row upon row of ships, with their furled white sails and colourful fluttering flags. Barges, punts and other boats moved back and forth between the majestic warships. Unlike his younger brother Charles, who charged about the house wearing a paper hat, menacingly waving anything remotely sword-like, Henry had no desire to join Nelson's navy. But to travel the world to see exotic places and fantastic creatures — that would be something.

Henry began to draw and imagine those faraway places. Tropical islands and deep dark forests. Mighty rivers and towering mountains. Time passed quickly, and it wasn't until he saw the state of the tide that he was roused from his reverie. It was ebbing strongly, and his little boat sat stranded, far from the water.

He felt a rising panic. Hastily, he began to stow his drawing and pencils. But he fumbled and dropped things. An overwhelming feeling of frustration swept over him. No matter how many times he put the paper and pencils away in the satchel, he looked down to see them on the ground in front of him. The wind rose. It picked up his drawing and blew it away from him. He started chasing it, first onto the beach and then out into the water. Deep mud sucked at his feet. He looked up towards the boat. Instead of a mudflat, the boat was stuck fast in ice. He looked down and he was knee-deep in snow. Then the cold started seeping through his bones and his teeth began to chatter. He heard a voice. At first, it sounded like his mother.

"Henry, Henry …"

Then it morphed into a man's deep tones.

"Mr Hellyer."

VAN DIEMEN'S LAND, NOVEMBER 1828

Henry's eyes sprang open. He was breathing fast, and his heart was racing. His eyes flitted back and forth looking for the boat, the island, his drawing. It took a moment for him to focus.

"Mr Hellyer, Sir, you was callin' out in your sleep."

Sandy McKay's rough hand rested gently on Henry's shoulder. It was daylight, but only just. Henry glanced around the tent's gloom. He took in his surroundings and his heart sank. He remembered where he was.

Outside, the icy wind whipped about with an evil ferocity. Snow lay piled at the mouth of the gap between the two massive boulders where they had pitched their tent. They were sheltering down in the deep canyon – Fury Gorge – Henry had named it two days earlier when they first descended into this awful chasm.

"You'll be pleased to know Sir, Cutts has got the fire goin'."

Henry sat up and McKay handed him a pannikin. Henry sipped at the hot, sweet black tea. Before he was half-done, the tea was cold.

"Mr Hellyer, Sir, we'd best make a start soon. I reckon it'll take us a good half-day to climb out of here, and then we must make our way around the Cradle. I remember Mr Fossey sayin' there's a valley with a lake to its north – that might afford us some shelter if the wind and snow was to come on again, like yesterday."

Henry nodded and passed the pannikin back to McKay, who continued.

"And Cutts is baking the last of the flour into a damper. It's not much for a man to march on, but maybe the dogs might catch us another badger or porcupine."

Henry frowned. They were still at least three days from the Surrey Hills stock hut. He'd been in a similar situation twenty months before, but without the dogs – or McKay. Lost and starving, engulfed in the dark tangled forests of the Arthur River valley. He and Cutts were lucky to survive.

Henry watched McKay back out of the tiny tent, in which the three men and two dogs had huddled together for warmth during the night. Henry opened his satchel, pulled out his journal and made brief notes on yesterday's travails and todays plans. As he did up the buckles, his fingers brushed across the curves of a daisy. He traced his index finger along the ridges and grooves. His heart ached.

They broke camp and followed the swollen river upstream, looking for a place to cross. With each hour the water-level rose further, swelled by the melting snow. They paused several times to survey a likely ford, but McKay shook his head and they trudged on. Keeping moving kept them warm; and no one relished wet clothes while the temperature hovered just above freezing.

After several hours, they came to a fallen tree that spanned the foaming torrent. McKay shouted above the roar of the water that this was the place. He stepped out onto the log and deftly walked across. Henry followed close behind, but with less sureness. He bent forward, trying to stabilise himself by holding onto broken limbs that protruded from the log at odd angles. He was almost across. Then he slipped. Henry plunged into the water and grabbed at a branch as he fell. The cold punched him in the chest, driving the breath out of him. He held on grimly. The current ripped at his body, threatening to sweep him away. McKay, who had one foot on the far bank, turned at this precise moment.

"Take my hand!" McKay bellowed over the roaring water.

Henry threw an arm towards him, but he lost his footing as he did so, and their hands missed. In a heartbeat, McKay reassessed the situation and snatched at the strap of the satchel over Henry's shoulder.

Cutts watched helplessly from the opposite bank, while McKay and Henry struggled. McKay held a small tree by one hand, the satchel strap in the other, while Henry dangled and flailed with the satchel pulled up into his arm pit. Water surged around Henry's chest, and occasionally over his head. McKay's grip on the sapling and the strength of the satchel's broad leather strap the only things between Henry and a watery oblivion.

Henry twisted his body, reached around, and grasped McKay's wrist. McKay let go of the strap and clamped his vice-like hand around Henry's wrist. With tendons and muscles straining, and stones spitting from under his feet, McKay dug in his heels and hauled Henry onto the bank. Both men tumbled down on the gravel, gasping for breath. Henry coughing, spluttering, and dripping wet.

At length, Henry regained his composure.

"Thank you, McKay. You saved me."

"Aye, that I did," laughed McKay, "but what would Mr Curr have to say, if I was to come back without ye?"

"Sometimes, I think he, and the Company, might be better off without me."

Henry rolled onto his back and stared up at the racing clouds and sighed deeply.

"What have we found on this expedition, or any of the ones before it? More mountains? I'm tired of naming mountains, McKay. Mountains and rivers and ravines and cascades. There is no Xanadu hidden beyond these peaks, no 'twice five miles of fertile ground'."

McKay looked at Henry quizzically, he knew Henry was quoting poetry, but didn't dare show his ignorance. Henry prattled on.

"Just more mountains, more gorges, more bogs, more desolate heath. When did we last see a native track? Or a hut, or signs of their burning? Even they do not come here. There is no game to be hunted. Neither sheep nor kangaroo can eat rocks and ice. The Lord has cast us adrift in the least hospitable land in all creation."

They sat silently for a time and watched Cutts inch his way across the log on his backside, a dog under each arm. McKay decided to change the subject.

"That fine bag of yours saved your life, as much as I did."

Henry looked down at his satchel then up at Sandy, the truth of McKay's statement stunned him.

The conversation ended abruptly, as Cutts approached to within earshot. The big man threw one dog, and then the other onto the bank and then hauled himself up. The dogs barked and wagged their tails furiously, as if to acknowledge the safe reunion of the party. Cutts was grinning from ear to ear.

The climb up the far side of the gorge was every bit as perilous as they'd imagined. They clawed their way up the precipitous slope, pulling themselves up by the spindly trunks and branches of the trees that clung precariously to the cliff faces. Often, it was so steep, the dogs needed to be carried or passed from man-to-man. When they rested, Henry dared not look down. The canyon floor was a dizzying quarter of a mile below them.

After hours of struggle, they eventually emerged from the gorge onto high ground, where the going was better. As the sun began to sink towards the horizon, they finally crested the high ridge northwest of the Cradle. Henry and Sandy paused to take in the view, while Cutts and the dogs forged on ahead, down the long slope, keen to make camp by the lake.

The wind had dropped, and the clouds had lifted. They stood atop the rim of a basin formed by rugged peaks, which terminated on their right with the jagged glory of the Cradle, its pinnacles and ledges dusted in snow. From their high vantage point, they looked down upon the exquisitely shaped body of water running north-south, its waist narrowing to curve around a promontory far below them.

Henry and McKay stood side-by-side for several minutes before Henry spoke.

"Mr Fossey's description does not do justice to this place."

McKay smiled, "If you pardon my sayin', Sir, if the Lord has cast us adrift, he's chosen a mightily pretty place to do it."

"Yes. He has," said Henry softly, "and McKay — Sandy, today has reminded me how I deeply value your strength. Your valour. Your … companionship."

They turned their attention to watching Cutts's descent. After a while Henry spoke again.

"If anything should happen to me, you should have this satchel — it was a gift from my mother. A symbol of love."

Silence settled between them. The last golden rays of the sun glinted off the mountain and a deep purple shadow crept across the lake.

"If you'll pardon me, Mr Hellyer, you're speakin' nonsense. You'll not come to any harm while I'm at hand."

"Soon, you won't be at hand, Sandy. Both Mr Fossey and I have written letters of reference to accompany your petition to the Governor for a ticket-of-leave. I have no doubt you'll get your freedom."

"Aye, maybe. But I'll not be counting my chickens. Mr Curr wrote me a fine letter last year and I'm still here."

Henry placed his arm around Sandy's broad shoulders.

"Well, today I am indeed glad of that!"

HOBART TOWN, SEPTEMBER 1832

Sandy walked down the long corridor of the Survey Department. He stopped outside Mr Calder's office, knocked and waited.

"Come!"

He opened the door and stepped across the threshold.

"You wanted to see me, Sir?"

"Ah, McKay. Yes." The Senior Government Surveyor fumbled about amongst his papers. "This arrived for you." He leaned forward across his desk and proffered a letter to Sandy.

Sandy was concerned. In his experience, letters rarely held good news. He took the envelope and looked at the front. He recognised his own name, but would need more time, and somewhere quiet, to decipher anything more. He turned it over. The wax seal was broken.

Calder cleared his throat, "Being aware of your capacity in this regard, I took the liberty of opening and reading it," he paused, "and I offer you my sincerest apologies. I should not have done so."

Sandy looked up and met Calder's eyes. Calder went on, "It arrived yesterday morning, and it was remiss of me not to pass it on at the time. But I, erm … became distracted by other matters."

"Yes, Sir."

"You would have heard, no doubt, that a gentleman, who you formerly served when you were assigned to the Van Diemen's Land Company, is due to join the department in the position of Assistant Surveyor."

"Yes, Sir, I've heard. I know Mr Hellyer well and I look forward to workin' with him again. He's a fine man. He'll be an asset to the department."

"Well, we can no longer expect him." Calder paused, his brow knitted.

"He is dead. The Surveyor General received the news from Mr Curr, the company's agent at Circular Head, informing him of the situation."

Sandy looked down at his feet, bewildered, his head swimming. And yet an understanding was already forming at the back of his mind.

"How?"

"Shot himself. Blew his brains out. It appears he was driven to the desperate act by the belief he was being slandered. Though, what these accusations were, or who was making them, no one can — or is willing to — say."

"And what's this to do with me, Sir?" Sandy asked quietly.

"This letter is from Mr Hellyer's brother, who lives here in town. Apparently, among Mr Hellyer's personal effects there is a valise, or something of the sort, he directed that you should have."

"Yes, Sir — a satchel."

. . .

AUTHOR'S NOTE — "The Satchel" is fiction, but the named characters are not. Nor is it fiction that, in the early hours of Sunday, September 2, 1832, the Van Diemen's Land Company's chief surveyor and architect, Henry Hellyer, committed suicide. His last written words, "Alas my mother, in an agony, I fly to my saviour".

DAVID WILSON is a writer, editor, flood forecaster and former school teacher. He writes under the name "E.regnans" at The Footy Almanac *and has stories in several books. He is married with two daughters and the four of them all live together with their dog, Pip, close to the Merri Creek in Melbourne. He suffered acquired brain injury and a broken C5 vertebra in a car accident in 1995 and is recovering alright. Favourite tree:* Eucalyptus regnans.

The ballad of Skull Callaghan

DAVID WILSON

It's early. The moon still hangs in the western sky as Skull Callaghan wakes to the sound of rustling. Skull's heeler, Swanny, shifts on his mat. The dog searches for warmth, but in the fireplace of last night only the ghosts of embers remain. Ghosts of logs, ghosts of warmth mock Swanny, lying curled into himself. The dog pulls himself tighter. Outside, the weakest of dawn's first light spills into the valley.

"Hmm. No rain, Swanny."

Skull Callaghan wakes on the couch; stiff and cold. It would seem that last night was another in a growing line of nights on which he fell asleep in front of the fire. Skull looks at the blanket across his legs; wonders from where it came. Through uncurtained windows, dawn's light softly advances into Skull Callaghan's simple house. It is a house without fanfare. A house without extravagance.

"Again."

The whole district is increasingly desperate for rain. Tanks are starting to run dry. But at least the winter is ahead of them.

"At least winter is ahead of us."

A magpie erupts with outrageous song. Swanny is roused and stands rapidly to attention, like a military figure on hearing the national anthem. Swanny's tail points straight back behind him. His nose twitches in the dawn light, his eyes sparkle with awareness. A second magpie drifts on the merest morning thermal, banks towards the house and lands quietly on the veranda. Swanny sees this, hears it; the hairs on Swanny's back stand up. He steps slowly, deftly, silently, towards the door, closed as it is; and maintains a line of sight with the trespassing magpie through the window, his movements controlled subconsciously by generations of instinct.

Skull notes Swanny's attention on something outside. It's enough to stop his wondering about the blanket ("Ahh, life is a mystery.")

"What's up, Swan? Do we have visitors?"

Silence from the dog.

"Ask them in, if they're good-looking," says Skull.

Silence stretches out before them, as familiar as hope.

Swanny stands like a statue.

This customary morning silence is welcome.

A quiet tap-tap-tapping starts up. Skull slowly stands and listens and as he does so, he stretches his arms to the roof. At the same time, Swanny begins a low, guttural growl of concentration. Something has his attention.

"Ahh, what is it Swanny?" Skull scratches his stubble, scratches his arse and turns to look in the same direction as Swanny. Towards the front window.

"Oh yes, mate. That's a magpie."

The magpie curiously pecks at Skull's elastic-sided boots which lie on the veranda.

"She's nothing to worry about, mate."

Skull rolls his head around his neck. "Carn," he says, "let's see this sunrise."

They both walk to the door. The metal handle is cold to touch. Outside, all is damp with dew.

. . .

Woodsmoke trails from chimneys. A low sky hangs close over ramshackle buildings, over the trees. The hills seem lost in cloud. Down in the valley, Sally is on duty at the General Store. The General Store, the town, as silent as a prayer.

Leaves of introduced European trees turn with the season; trees that line the main street. Road and footpath both already lie under a patchy, thin blanket of the fallen. This day, Skull feels moisture in the air. His hair is damp as he stumps up the step of the store.

"G'day S Callaghan," says Sally, as Skull pushes through the doorway.

"Sally, how are yeh?"

"Ahh, not bad, Skull. Mick placed your club order out the back last night. Do you want to grab it yourself?"

Sally gestures through a doorway behind her. The doorway leads to a storeroom and, further on, to a separate building; to living quarters for Sally and Mick; long-time proprietors of the General Store and post office.

"Righto. I will. That's a terrific fire."

Sally has a roaring fire dancing in the corner.

"Thanks, I set it last night. You know I like to be prepared," she says.

"You and me both," says Skull, following Sally out to the bitterly cold storeroom.

As they stand lost amongst packaging, containers and labels, Skull marvels at the possibility of it all. From this very room, from this very spot, he could send any item of his possession to another human, anywhere on the Earth. The sense of it hits him. The size of it.

"What's the furthest you've ever sent something by post, Sally?" he asks.

"What's that? Oh, here's the order, Skull. For the footy club."

"Great. Sal, what's the furthest you've ever sent a package?"

"Oooh, let's see … probably to Dublin, to Ireland," she says. "Why?"

Leaves and thin branches of a gum tree scrape slowly, repeatedly, against the corrugated iron roof. A gum nut falls.

"Did it arrive safely?" Skull asks.

"I think so. Why would it not?" says Sally.

"Oh … no reason," says Skull. He has never had itchy feet. Skull collects the dozens of sausages, the bread, sauce. He collects medical tape; provisions for the footy club. "It's a kind of magic."

Sally smiles with half of her mouth. Skull turns to leave.

"Hey Skull," she says. "Any word?"

"Nah," he says, over his shoulder. He carries the provisions through the door and onto the street.

. . .

The home team has won the reserves match. Skull pats some of these old blokes on the back. So many old blokes. Many of them will play again now in the seniors. There are not enough players, not enough young ones. It's as if a generation has been lost. Skull himself has had to act as timekeeper, interchange steward and canteen operator this very morning. For starters. It's a full plate for the president of a club in hard times.

Before the senior game begins there is a brief respite. No, not really. There is no rest.

"Hey Thommo," says Skull.

"Hey Skull-man."

"How's your arm, old mate?"

Thommo stands with his arm in a sling. Clouds hang low over the valley; move slowly to the east. At the canteen, Julia and Ash serve bread rolls and cheese, soft drinks and chocolate. Customers take their rolls to the barbecue, where Maryanne gives them a sausage.

"Should be right. Couple of weeks, I reckon," says Thommo.

Skull knows about injury and he knows about the shifty shadow of luck. About how swiftly and suddenly the curtain can be pulled down.

"Good man. Could you manage the scoreboard today?"

The scoreboard is on the far side of the ground, over by the river. Usually, Ron looks after scoreboard duties. But Ron was spending the weekend on the mainland, seeing his daughter's kids.

"Ahh, Skull … I was hoping to get away at half time …"

"No worries, Thommo. Look, you score the first half. We'll find someone. Thanks mate."

. . .

To the west, a single shaft of sunlight angles through cloud as if the footy clubrooms themselves are the focal point of a Renaissance painting. Sunlight strikes the clubroom window. Moments later, the late afternoon sun dips behind the range, leaving only the diffuse scattered light of the everyday. Individual eucalypts stand as silhouettes against the flaming sky. Individuals among thousands of eucalypts on these slopes of living history.

So young. These opposition guys filing past; so young.

"Good work, Skull. Thanks mate."

Above, the undersides of clouds are sprayed with a spectrum of orange, somehow deepening to purple. Skull shuffles out from under the pavilion roof. Looks up. Drinks it in.

A mob of opposition players and officials knock past him, making for their cars.

"Can't stay, Skull. Catch you next time."

The sky will only appear aflame like this for a minute. Maybe two. And with the conviction of the dammed, Skull casts his eyes hungrily skywards. A strange awareness is upon him that this could be his last sunset.

"You blokes were pretty sharp today, Skull. Better luck next week, eh?"

The full moon rises in the east, crests a ridge.

An echo of laughter erupts from deep inside the changing rooms.

. . .

It's late. The tyres on Dimma's car crunch gravel as he slips from reverse into first. Back at the clubroom door Skull hears the flick of stones on car undercarriage and he smiles. Today Dimma had played a beauty in a losing side.

A break in the cloud now reveals the mighty full moon, high in her trajectory across the night sky; her light illuminates the entire valley. From the clubroom doorway, Skull has a clear view across the oval, across the other side of the river, across the small floodplain. There are no electric lights to be seen.

"Look at that, Swanny," he says, as he gingerly sits on the concrete step.

Man and dog sit alone on the steps outside the clubrooms; clubrooms which currently require a great deal of heavy and sustained effort in order to be cleaned and packed up; locked up.

They each gaze into the wilderness, mute.

Stars turn overhead.

Eventually, Skull clears his throat. "I don't know, mate. I don't know how much longer we can keep doing this," he says.

Across the valley, ancient trees stand silent and firm.

Skull picks up a stone; flicks it across the concrete apron of the clubrooms.

Swanny senses the mood. He breaks his attention from the distant river, stands and stretches his body. Swanny steps lightly in a small circle and swishes his tail before sitting back on the step. He looks at Skull.

"What are we gonna do, eh?"

Across the river, the ancient trees lean in, lean out.

. . .

Headlights sweep across the house as Skull Callaghan turns his ute up the long bush driveway. In the rear-vision mirror and to each side, all is dark and darker. Cones of high-beam light leap about as the ute passes over undulations in the drive. Up ahead, the kitchen light shines brightly through the window.

"What's this, Swan? Did you leave the light on?"

Swanny lies curled up on the passenger seat. In the foot well, partially used rolls of medical tape, drink bottles and half a loaf of sliced white bread bounce lightly as Skull eases the ute over the last of the potholes. He pulls on the handbrake and shuts down the engine. Silence roars in through the open window, the silence of millennia, and takes both man and dog. In the valley, not a leaf stirs.

"Hmm. Don't reckon it was me."

Skull looks at Swanny with a half-smile. The rapidly cooling engine ticks under a vault of stars. Some way off, a small branch falls from high in a canopy. Skull sits in the driver's seat and looks up at the moon. His phone rings.

"Hmm."

The phone lies on the dashboard. Skull reaches for it and turns it over to read the screen.

"It's Jimmy."

On the screen, he touches the green icon to accept the incoming call.

"Hey Jimmy," he says.

"Hi Dad."

Jimmy lives on the mainland now with his mum and with his sisters.

"How are you, mate? You OK?"

"Yeah, I'm OK."

Jimmy comes to stay with his dad every couple of weeks. Just for a weekend, usually.

"Good."

"Yeah."

"That's good."

"Yeah."

Skull reaches for a lever beside him and pulls it to recline the backrest of his seat by a few degrees.

"What are you up to?"

"Oh, not much."

"Uh-huh."

"Yeah … Just … Stuff."

There is no rhythm to Jimmy's conversations these days. It's hard. No. It's perfect. Skull thinks it is perfect.

"Righto," says Skull. "Stuff."

There is a lengthy pause before Jimmy continues.

"Yeah … what about you …? What are you up to?"

"Oh … well … sitting in the car with Swanny. We just got home."

"Oh yeah …?"

Fingers of cold snake their way through the open window of the car and around Skull's exposed skin. Skull's wrists feel cold.

"Yeah. Home from the footy. Got pumped."

"Oh."

"Yeah. You didn't miss much."

"OK."

With his free hand, Skull softly pats the dog beside him.

"Oh. Except the sunset. Yeah. The sunset was a real beauty. You would have loved it."

"Yeah."

"Yeah."

Eyes adjusted, Skull Callaghan looks around at the moonlit surrounds, at the shadows. He marvels at the definition of these moon-shadows cast by logs, by tussock grasses, by undulations on the ground.

Silence resounds deep between father and son.

"Dad?"

"Yes, mate."

A pause hangs in the darkness.

"Nah … it's nothing."

Skull closes his eyes. He continues to softly pat Swanny.

"Ahh. That's OK, Jimmy."

Skull looks towards his house and towards that kitchen light. It feels like only yesterday that he had parked the ute here and looked up to see his beautiful bride framed in the light of that window. There were years of arriving home in the dark like this. Years of arriving home to his family. A family that she had tended like a shepherd.

"Jimmy … it's great to hear your voice."

"Yeah, … yours too, Dad."

Darkness and distance hold father and son together in silence. With one hand Skull rubs his chin and then runs it through his thick and dirty hair.

"Dad?"

"Yes, mate."

"I'm gonna go."

Skull Callaghan holds the pose. One hand with the phone to his ear, the other rests flat against his head. Tufts of dark and greying and curling hair poke through his fingers.

"Righto, Jimmy. See you soon."

"OK."

Skull opens his eyes and looks out through the window of his car. He tries to imagine where Jimmy is right now. The skin at the back of his neck starts to itch.

"Jimmy ... I love you."

"... I love you, too, Dad."

Skull Callaghan waits for Jimmy to hang up the call. He presses his fingers into his scrunched-up eyes and as he does so, Skull slowly exhales the lonely wind of a forgotten valley. Through the familiar prism of a suspended tear, he turns to look at Swanny curled on the seat beside him.

In the kitchen window, ghosts of family play out their scene.

All is still.